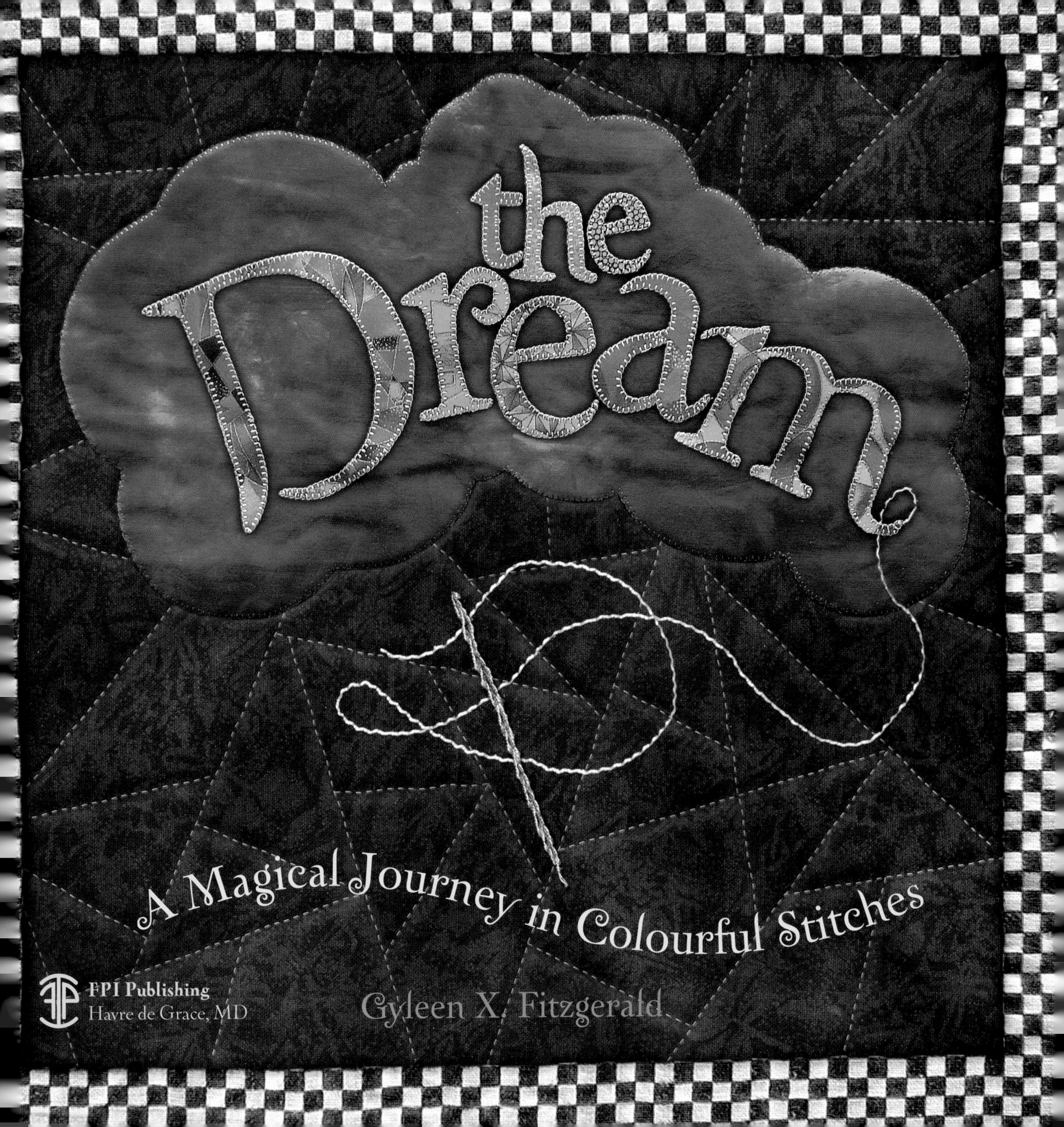
the Dream
A Magical Journey in Colourful Stitches
FPI Publishing
Havre de Grace, MD
Gyleen X. Fitzgerald

The Dream
by Gyleen X. Fitzgerald

Published by FPI Publishing
PO Box 247, Havre de Grace, MD 21078
www.ColourfulStitches.com

Cover and interior design by Pneuma Books, LLC
visit www.pneumabooks.com for more information.

**Publisher's Cataloging-In-Publication Data
(Prepared by The Donohue Group, Inc.)**

Fitzgerald, Gyleen X.
    The dream : a magical journey in colourful stitches / Gyleen X.
Fitzgerald.

    p. : ill. ; cm.
    ISBN-13: 978-0-9768215-1-9
    ISBN-10: 0-9768215-1-6

1. Quilting—Juvenile fiction. 2. Quiltmakers—Juvenile fiction. 3.
Quilts—Juvenile fiction. 4. Quilting—Patterns. 5. Quilting—
Fiction. 6. Quiltmakers—Fiction. 7. Quilts—Fiction 8. Quilting—
Patterns. 9. Fairy tales I. Title.

PS3556.I83   D74 2005
813.6/083   LCCN: 2005925353

10 09 08 07 06 05   6 5 4 3 2 1

The Dream is a special gift to:

----

by:

----

date:

To James for always believing in my dreams.

Why not always dream
As easy as water boils?
Let our spirits soar!

Table of Contents

Chapter 1

The Quilt Shop

"Aunt Hattie? Did you get any new fabric in last week?" asked twelve-year-old Hanna. Hanna was spending the afternoon in her Aunt Hattie's quilt shop, the only quilt shop in the county.

"New fabric? What do I need new fabric for? We have plenty right here."

"But Aunt Hattie! It all looks the same. Calico, calico, calico. Gray, gray, gray. You know I have some wild ideas for quilts. And I need lots of colours to quilt them."

"Well, I don't know where you get your ideas, Hanna. I suggest you stick to traditional quilting first. Learn the basics. You'll need a firm foundation if you're actually going to make those wild quilts someday."

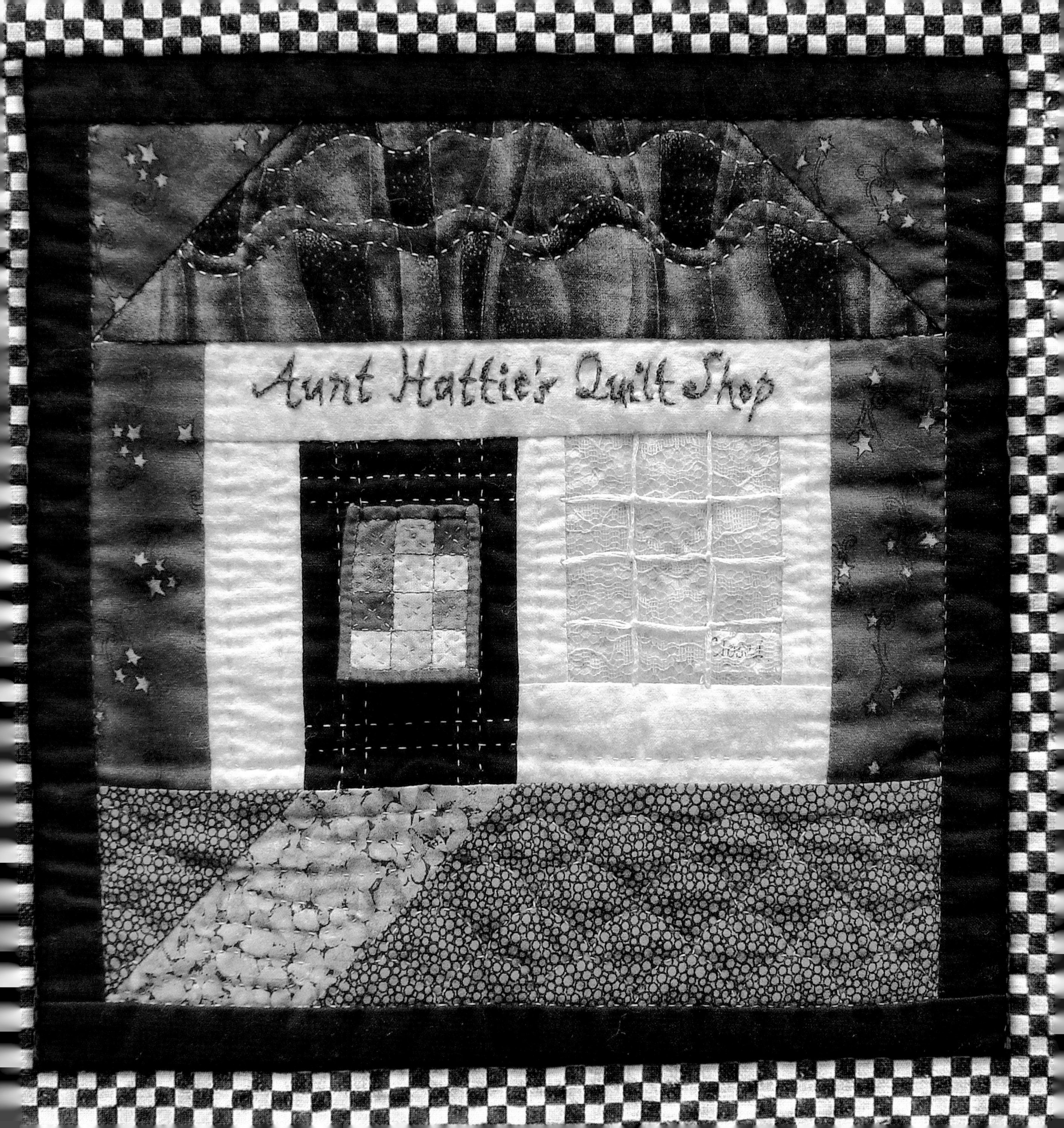
Aunt Hattie's Quilt Shop

"Oh, Aunt Hattie!"

Hanna gave up on the conversation and settled down in a warm corner of the shop. *Who wants to quilt with gray calico fabric? Who would use it if they had any choice?* Hanna's thoughts swirled. The fact is that Hanna's thoughts were always swirling with new fabrics and ideas for quilts. She pulled out her sketchbook and pencils and got to work on a new design for a quilt — one with plenty of colour.

Chapter

2

The Dream

Hanna hadn't gotten far on her sketch when she fell asleep under her favorite quilt. Maybe it was the shop, maybe it was her frustration with Aunt Hattie, but Hanna dreamed of fabric. Swatches of fabric in all colours, designs, and shapes fell on her like snow. When she tried to wipe her face, she realized her arms were full of bolts of fabric and she dropped it all on the floor. That brought the Good Fairy Gadget rushing to her side.

"Oh, my dear, my dear. Let me help you with all of these beautiful fabrics," she said as she gathered the bolts off of the floor. "Now, what is the trouble, dear?"

"I want to make bright, colourful quilts that express my thoughts and feelings."

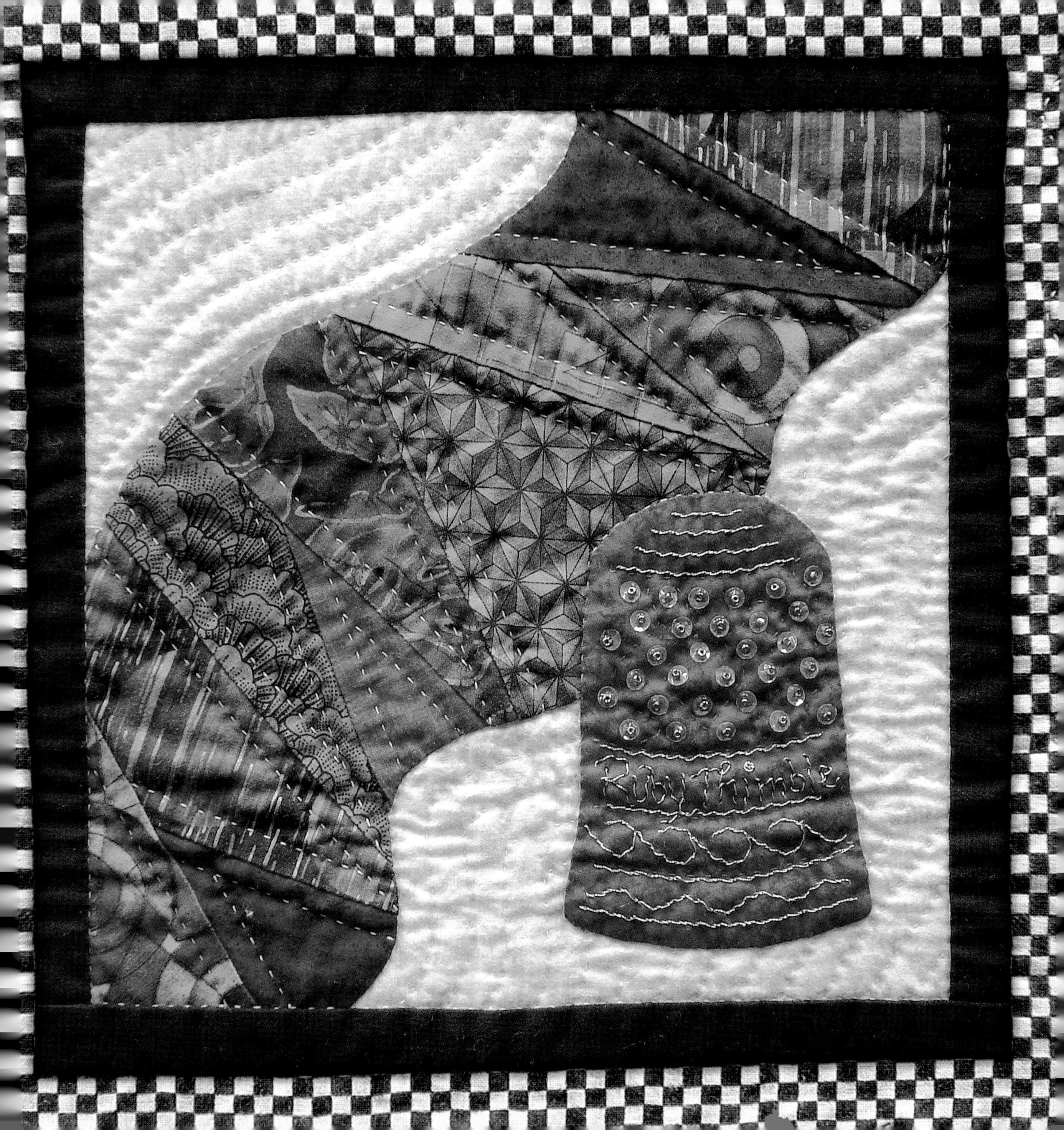
Ruby Thimble

"Wonderful!" exclaimed the Good Fairy Gadget.

"That sounds like a fantastic idea."

"But I don't have what it takes," said Hanna.

"Don't worry, my dear. You will. Come here and let me give you a hug." The Good Fairy Gadget opened her arms and hugged Hanna tightly. "Take this ruby thimble. It will protect your finger on your adventure."

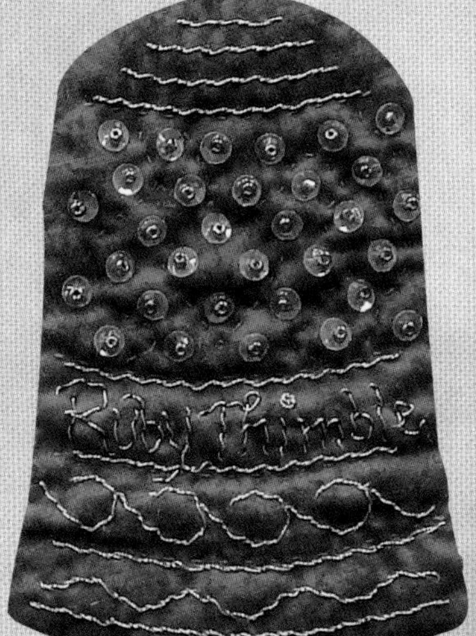
Ruby Thimble

"What adventure?" asked Hanna.

"You need some inspiration, Hanna, so an adventure is in order. Follow the Fabric Road and you will find all the inspiration you need."

Chapter

3

The Partner

Hanna grasped the ruby thimble tightly in her hand. She hadn't planned on adventure and she was happy that her dog Bobbin was with her. They had been walking for a while and Hanna was getting hungry. When they passed a field of Corn and Beans, she noticed a woman busy making dinner.

It would have been impossible *not* to see this woman. She had wild, colourful hair, and Hanna could not tell where the road ended and the woman's hair began. Hanna approached her carefully — she didn't want to startle the woman.

"Hello," called Hanna in a gentle voice.

"Oh my, hello. What a surprise! I don't get many visitors here."

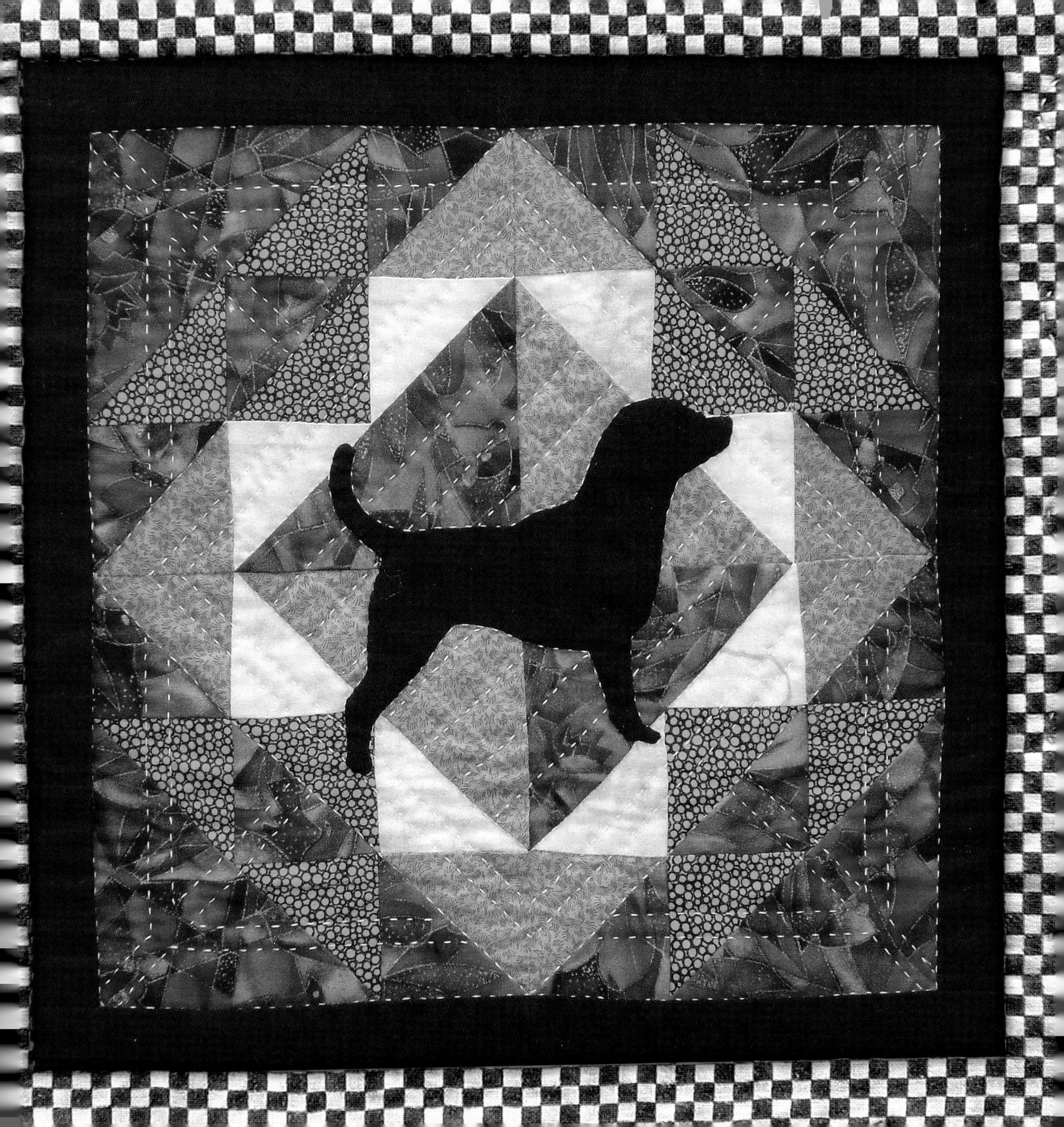

"Why not?!" exclaimed Hanna.

"Well, everyone teases me for being different. I don't have any style."

"What do you mean?"

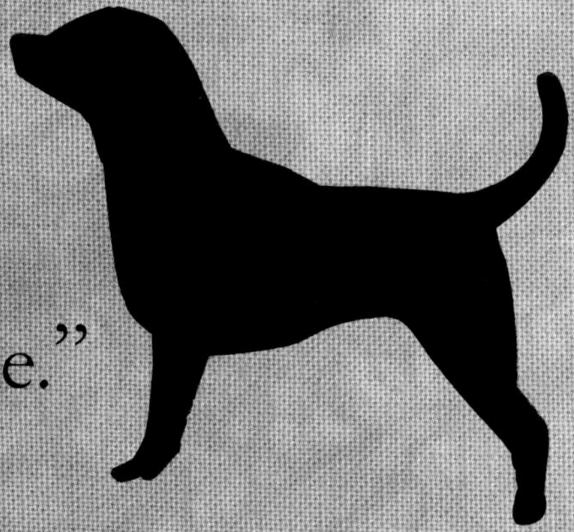

"Nothing matches or coordinates with me."

Hanna could see this was true. Corn and beans are not exactly hamburgers and french fries.

"Come with me," said Hanna. "I am looking for inspiration at the end of the road, and I'm sure that we'll find style there."

So the lady became Hanna's partner.

Chapter 4

The Rescue

The countryside was textured with stripes, checks, and geometrics. The Fabric Road was turning rough and wrinkled (the sizing hadn't been washed out yet). Hanna was getting scared. The road entered a forest and Hanna and the Partner came upon something like a log cabin. "What is this?" asked the Partner.

Hanna looked around to make sure no one would hear her critique and she saw a sewing machine Repairwoman running toward them. "Do you live here?" Hanna asked.

"Yes," said the Repairwoman, looking a bit annoyed. "Have you seen my oil can?"

"No," answered Hanna and the Partner in unison.

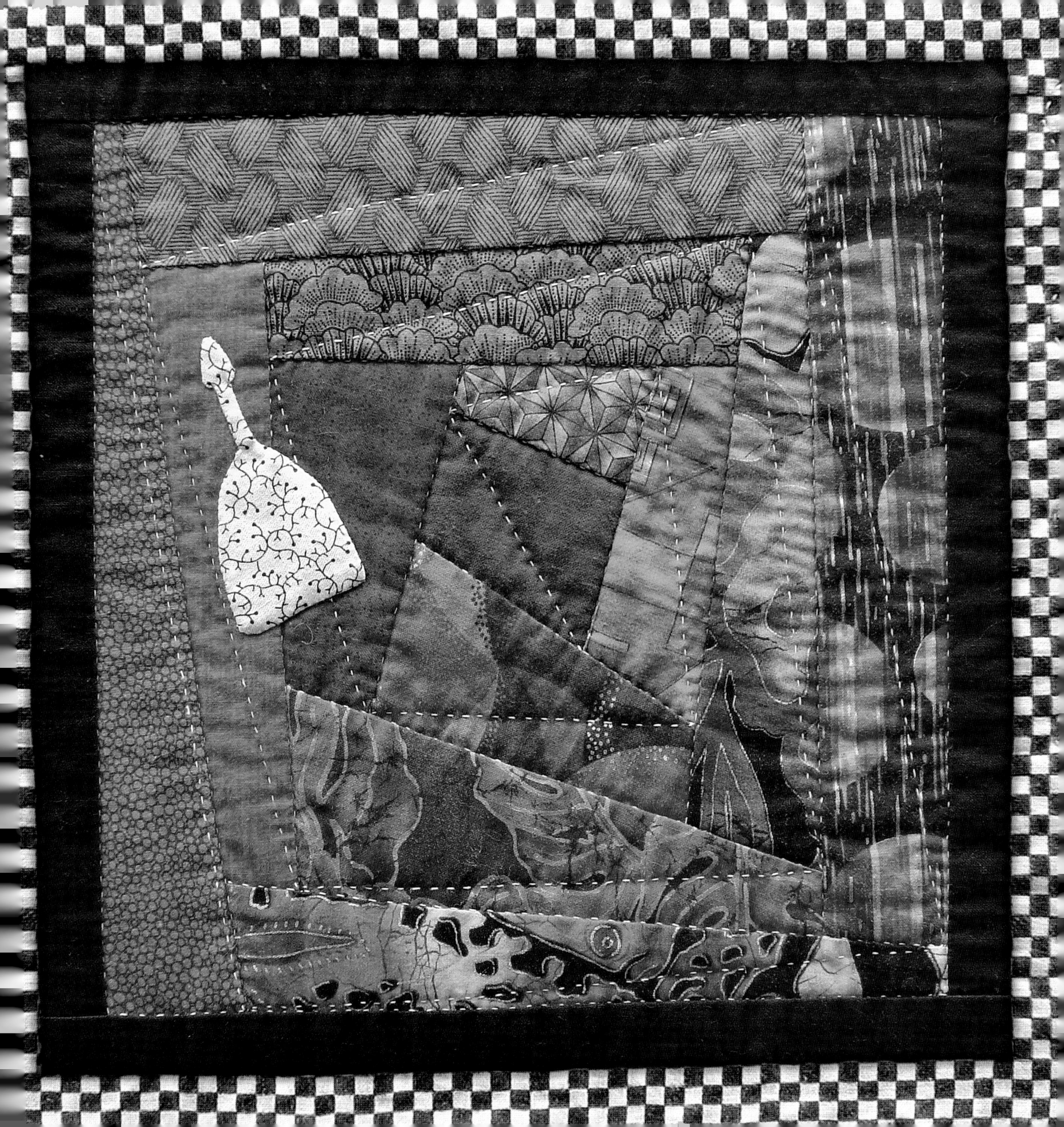

"This is a disaster," said the Repairwoman. "I need my oil can. Just look at my log cabin! I can't get the logs straight. My machine needs oil."

Hanna thought the problem might be with the person using the machine and not the machine itself, but she decided not to say so. The Partner asked, "Do you think the oil will rescue your cabin?"

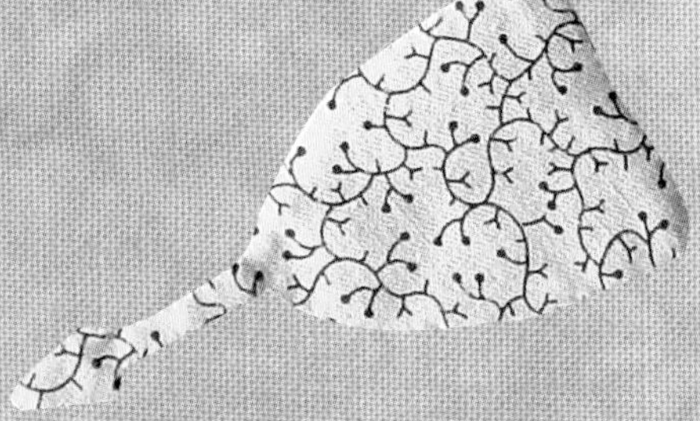

"I hope so," said the Repairwoman.

"Well, why don't you come with us?" Hanna asked. "We're following the Fabric Road. I'm looking for inspiration and the Partner is looking for style. Maybe we can find your oil can too."

So together, Bobbin, Hanna, the Partner, and the Repairwoman set off down the Fabric Road.

Chapter 5

The Forest

The road through the forest had not been pressed, so the going was slow. Bobbin sniffed the trail, and Hanna stuck by his side. But she stopped cold when she saw Bobbin sniffing a Bear's Paw print.

"Oh no!" exclaimed the Partner. "We'll never make it to the end of the road. Where's the Bear?"

They all stopped and looked around. Hanna noticed a shadow behind one of the trees and yelled, "The Bear!"

"Wait!" called the Bear. "Please, don't run. I won't hurt you. I'm just a little bashful. I saw you at the cabin and I wanted to join in, but…"

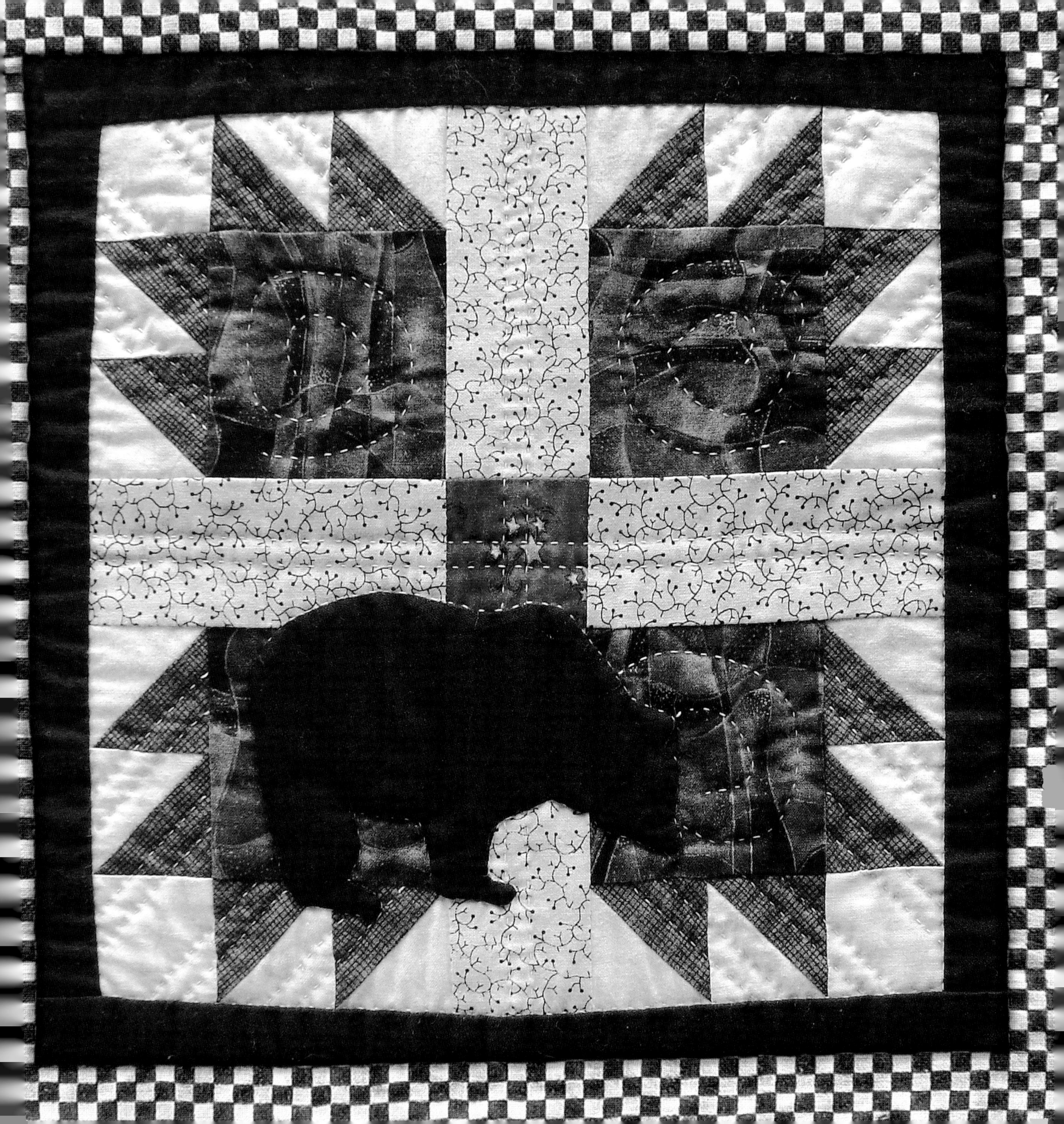

The Bear's voice trailed off. The Bear was so bashful that she couldn't even bear down hard enough to set a decent paw print.

"What are you doing here? You scared us!" said Hanna.

"I was looking for a Bee. I thought maybe you had one."

Hanna had seen many interesting things along the Fabric Road, but no bees. Now here was a bashful Bear looking for a Bee.

"Unfortunately I don't have a Bee for you. But we're all traveling down the Fabric Road to find what we need. Join us if you'd like. Perhaps you'll find your Bee."

Chapter 6

The Vision

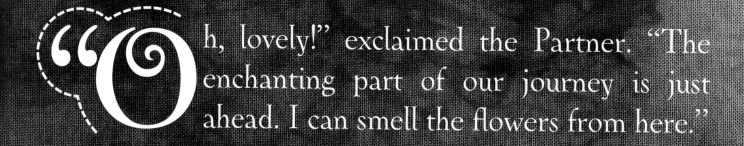

"Oh, lovely!" exclaimed the Partner. "The enchanting part of our journey is just ahead. I can smell the flowers from here."

As the group emerged from the forest, Hanna wished for sunglasses. A great field of wildflowers spread out at her feet. "These are beautiful. Look at the colours!" she yelled.

Bobbin ran wild, leaving a trail of petals in his wake. The Partner felt at home among the vivid colours. "Let's stop and pick some flowers for your basket," she suggested to Hanna.

"That's a wonderful idea," said Hanna. "Isn't it strange how there are so many colours, but they all come together? Nature has such style."

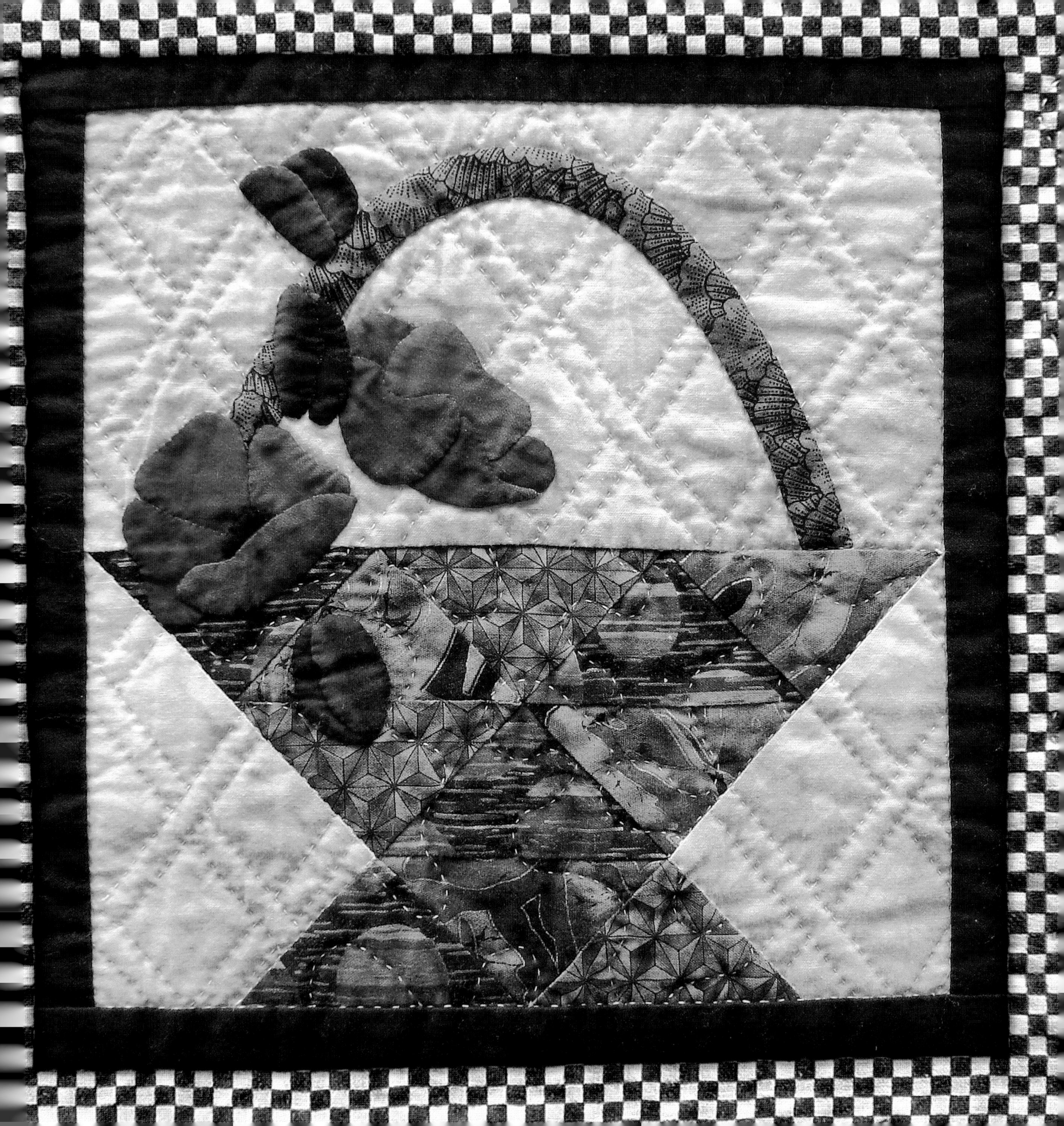

"Absolutely," said the Partner. "I agree."

Hanna and the Partner filled the basket with wildflowers, and the Partner was struck with an idea. "Can I help you hand-dye your fabric?"

Hanna had never thought of working with a partner before. She liked the idea, and without even knowing it, she started to hum the tune to a song.

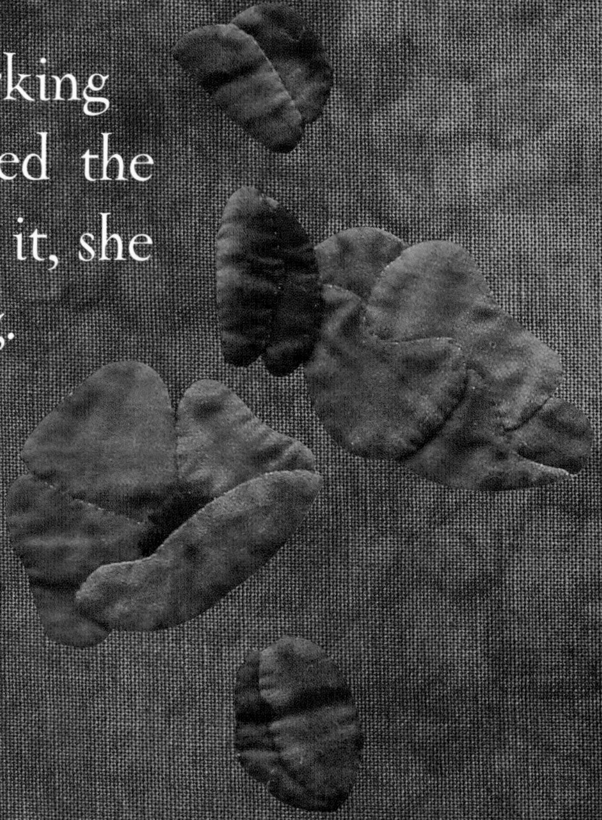

Chapter

7

The Crossroads

Hanna and her friends pressed onward. Each was eager to find what they were looking for. When road signs appeared, they knew they were close. The signs directed visitors where they needed to go. Fat Quarters this way! Batiks that way! Hand-dyes this way! Vendors here!

"This must be the Paducah Crossroads," Hanna said. "But where are the quilt artists? Where is inspiration? And the oil can? Where is the Bee? Where is style? What is Paducah, anyway?"

"Did someone call me?" asked the Judge.

"Call you? No, I don't think so," said Hanna.

"Well, yes, yes you did, young lady. My name is Paducah, and only quilt artists cross these roads."

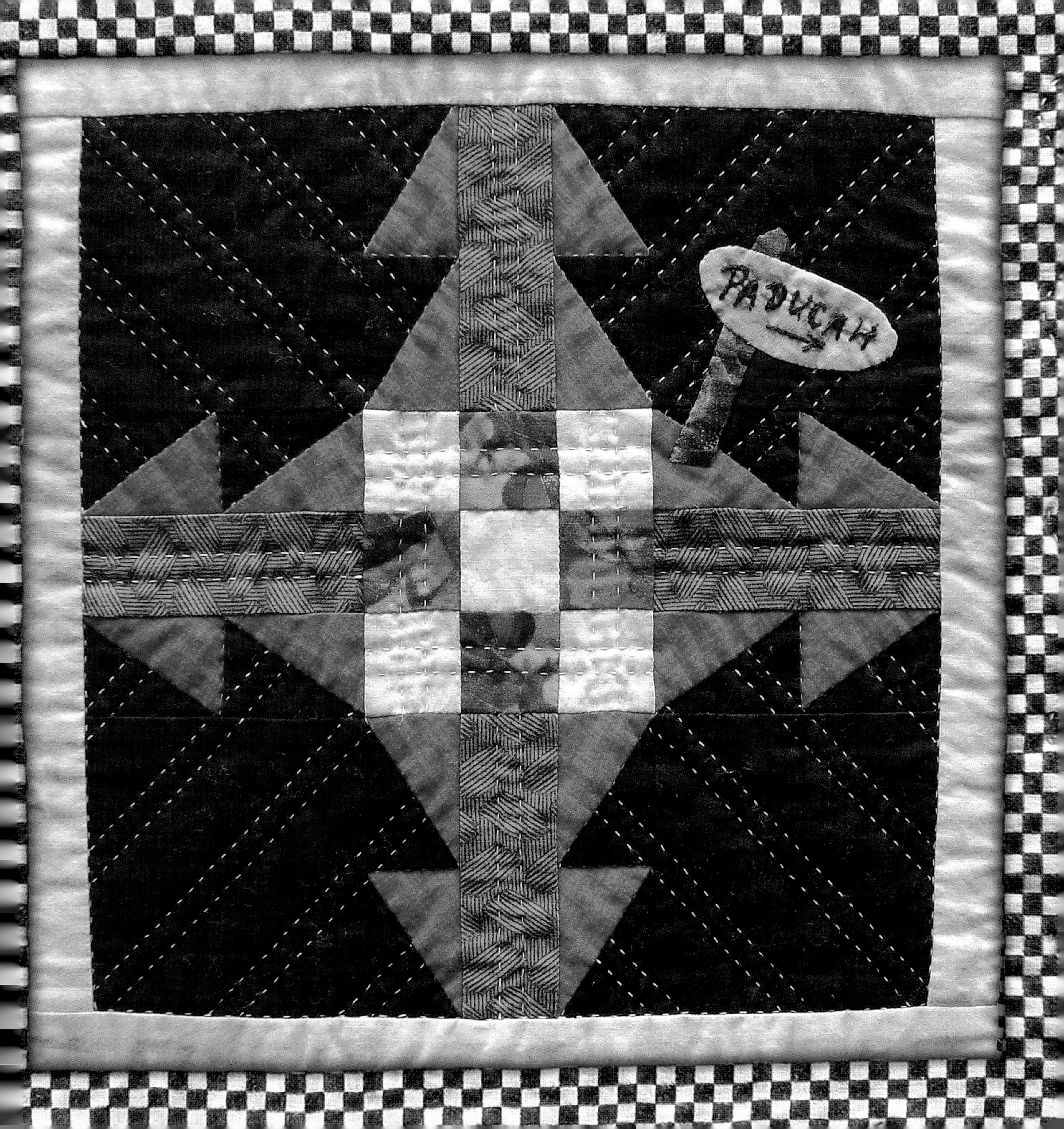
PADUCAH

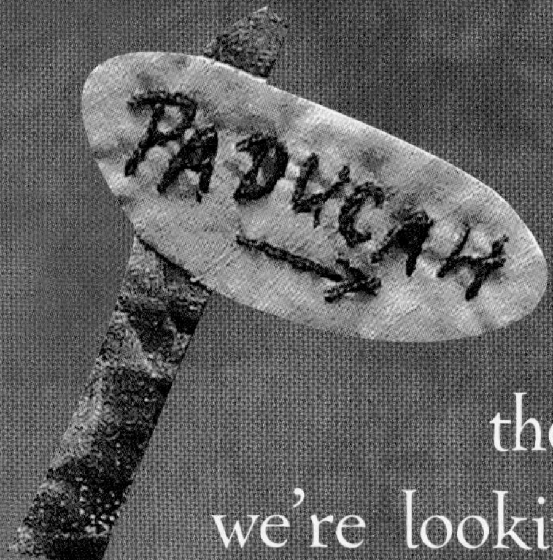
PADUCAH

"No!" exclaimed Hanna, and she started to cry. "That just can't be. We must cross these roads because we have not found what we're looking for. But I'm no quilt artist, and my friends aren't either."

"Hmmm," said Paducah. "What are you looking for?"

Hanna spoke up for everyone and Paducah listened.

"Well, it sounds to me like you must visit the Spool Witch," said Paducah. "She keeps the golden thread. To be a great quilt artist you must know how to do thread play. And believe me, the golden thread will be a wonderful source of inspiration."

Paducah turned away from the group with a wave. "Good luck! May you find what you're looking for!"

Chapter

8

The Witch

"I'm not so sure about looking for a witch," said Hanna as they continued along the Fabric Road into the woods.

"I hope she doesn't want to talk with me," said the Bear.

"Oh, don't worry, you two," said the Partner. "Bobbin and the Repairwoman are right here with us."

It wasn't long before they found the Spool Witch in her studio among the forest's fibers. She certainly didn't look willing to give them anything.

"What do you want?" asked the witch, and she didn't sound like she really wanted to know.

"I've come in search of inspiration and golden thread," said Hanna.

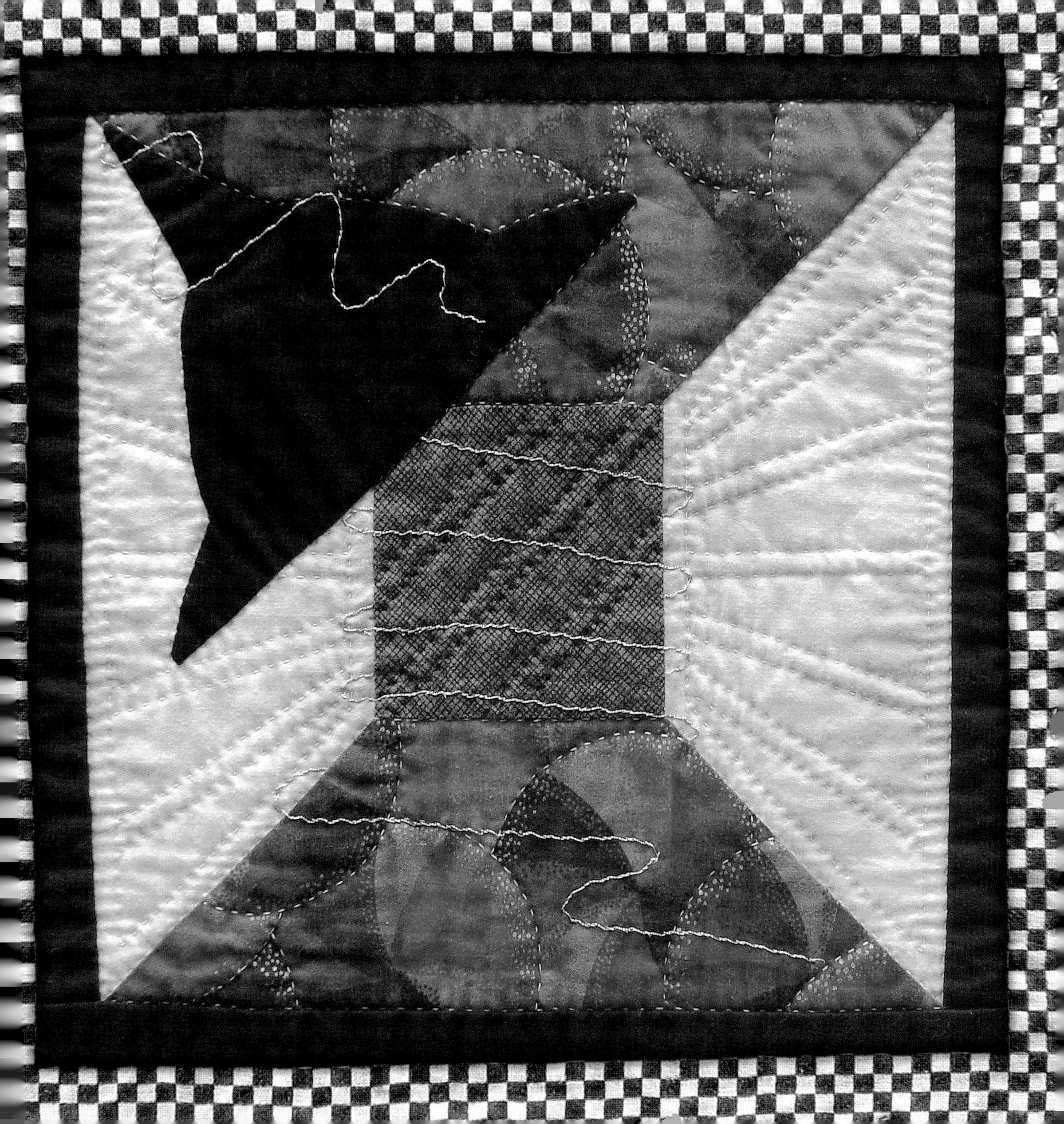

Hanna could see Spool Witch had plenty of thread. It was all over the studio. But the only golden thread was entwined in her cloak, which looked like a work of art.

"I have no golden thread for you or anyone else. Now off you go. All of you! I have work to do," said the witch. She turned away from them in a flurry and sent buttons and thread flying about.

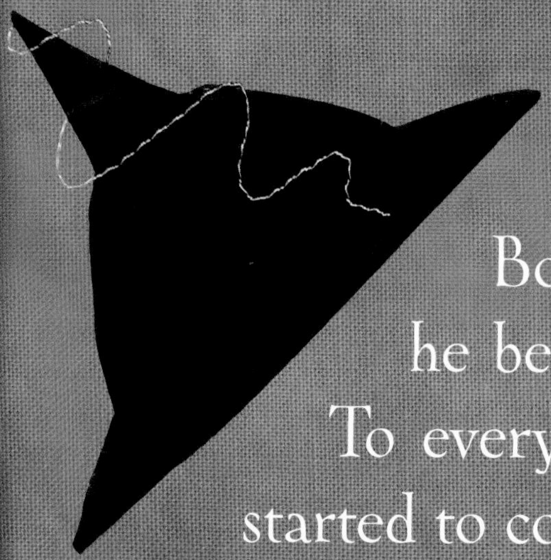

Bobbin did not like the witch's reply and he began to run in circles around the witch. To everyone's great surprise, the Spool Witch started to come unwound.

"Run, Bobbin! Run!" they all shouted.

Bobbin was now filled with golden thread, and Hanna knew that inspiration was close.

Chapter
9

The Short Cut

hey ran from the studio with thread trailing behind them. They had run in so many circles that they weren't certain how to get back to the crossroads. Hanna felt herself filling up with ideas. "Oh, wow!" she exclaimed to her friends. "I'm ready to design something!"

To herself she thought, *I wonder if the Repairwoman will let me use her sewing machine to make my quilt. After all, we're friends now.* But Hanna also knew that friendship could be broken over the misuse of a featherweight.

The friends spotted a clearing in the forest. "A short cut!" yelled the Partner, and they all rushed on to the clearing.

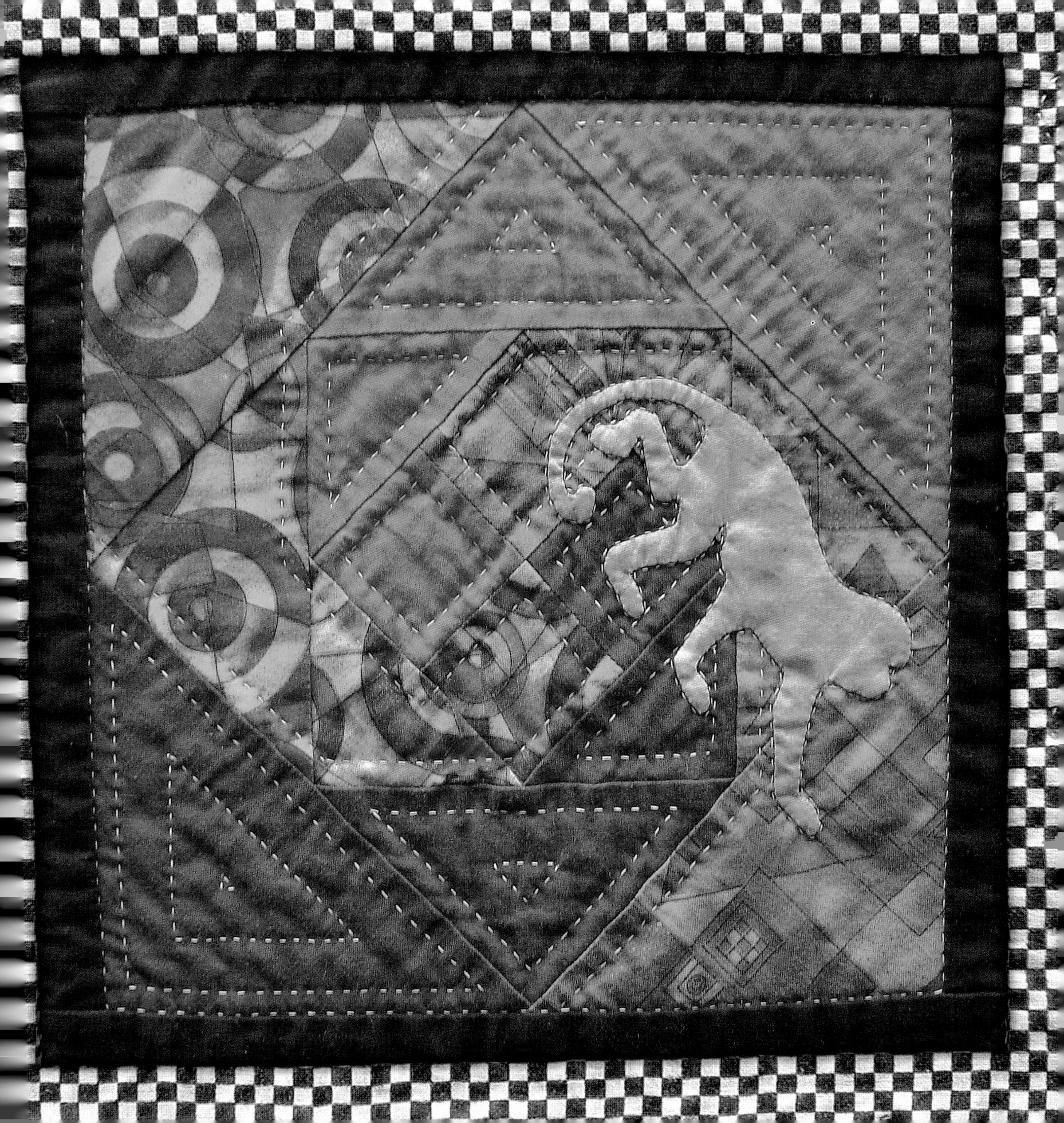

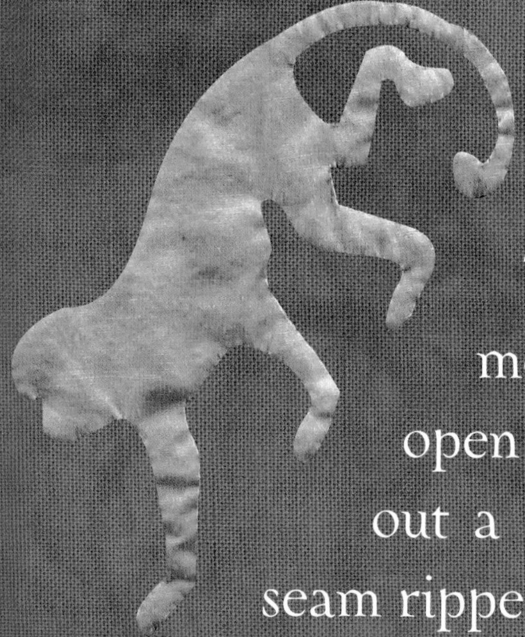

The Bear got there first. She stopped abruptly and then slowly approached a small black box. The friends joined her and Hanna motioned to the Repairwoman to open the box. The Repairwoman pulled out a stiletto, a screwdriver, and even a seam ripper, but nothing opened the box.

"Think," urged Hanna. "Think outside the box."

In a last ditch effort, the Repairwoman pulled out a wrench and successfully opened the box. Inside they found a needle case, which contained a silver needle. Hanna put the needle in her pocket, and no one even noticed the monkey running off with the wrench.

Chapter
10

The Spill

Finally Hanna said what all of them were thinking: "Why haven't we reached the crossroads yet? I don't think it took this long to reach the witch's studio."

"I don't think so," said the Bear, "and I must stop to rest. I haven't eaten in hours and I can't go another step."

They stopped and sat down beneath a huge tree full of blossoms. Bees! "Here are my Bees!" exclaimed the Bear, and she found the strength to climb the tree.

"You're too big!" yelled the Repairwoman. "You'll break the branches and fall."

The Bear *was* too big and with a sharp crack, the branch broke and oil started spilling from the break.

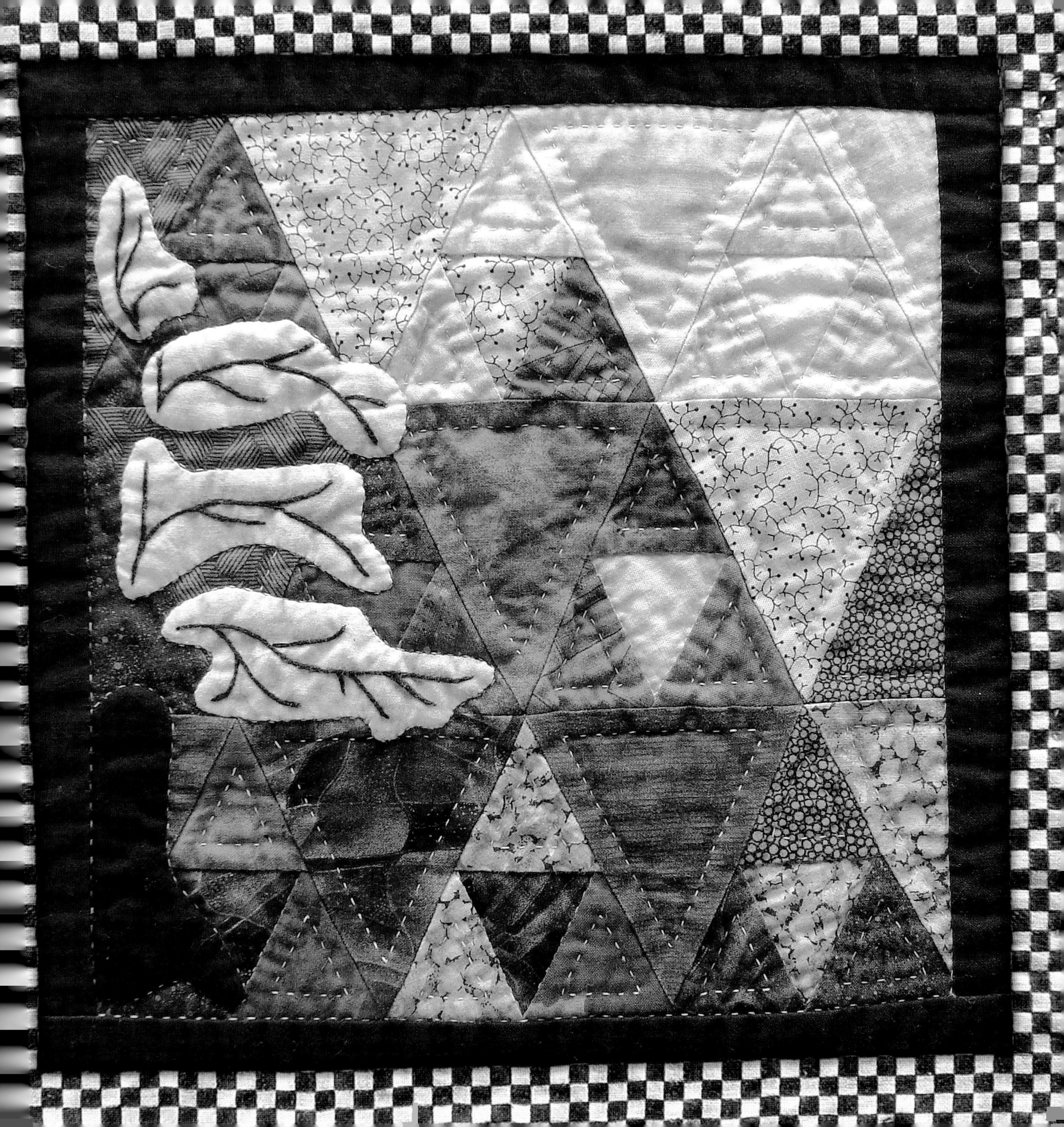

"Hurry," said the Repairwoman. "Find something to absorb the oil."

"Not my fabric," said Hanna.

The Partner picked some of the blossoms from the fallen branch and layered them on top of the oil.

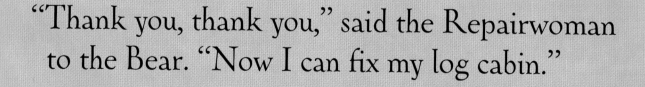

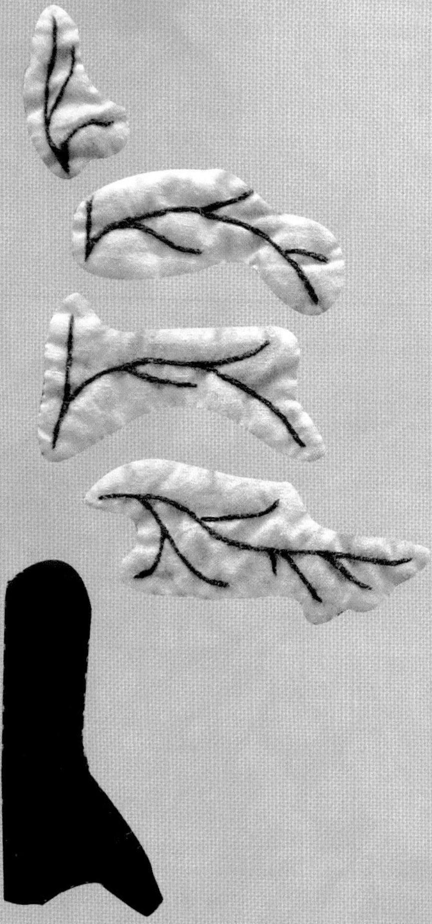

"Look," said Hanna. "The blossoms absorb oil just like batting."

"Thank you, thank you," said the Repairwoman to the Bear. "Now I can fix my log cabin."

"Can I use your machine?" asked Hanna.

At that request, the Bear hid in the blossoms.

Chapter
11

The Silence

There are many ways to build a good friendship, but lending sewing machines is not one of them. The group walked in silence for a while, and finally Hanna said, "Just kidding."

When they saw the crossroads ahead, the group increased the rhythm of their steps until they were almost running. No one noticed the ripped seam in the road until it was too late. Hanna was the first to fall, then the Partner, followed by the Repairwoman, and finally the Bear.

Bobbin barked in amusement at the pile up. As the Partner lay on the forest floor, she noticed something sparkling in the open seam. "Broken China," she said out loud — to herself. Then she said, "Hey everyone, someone has sewn broken china into the road."

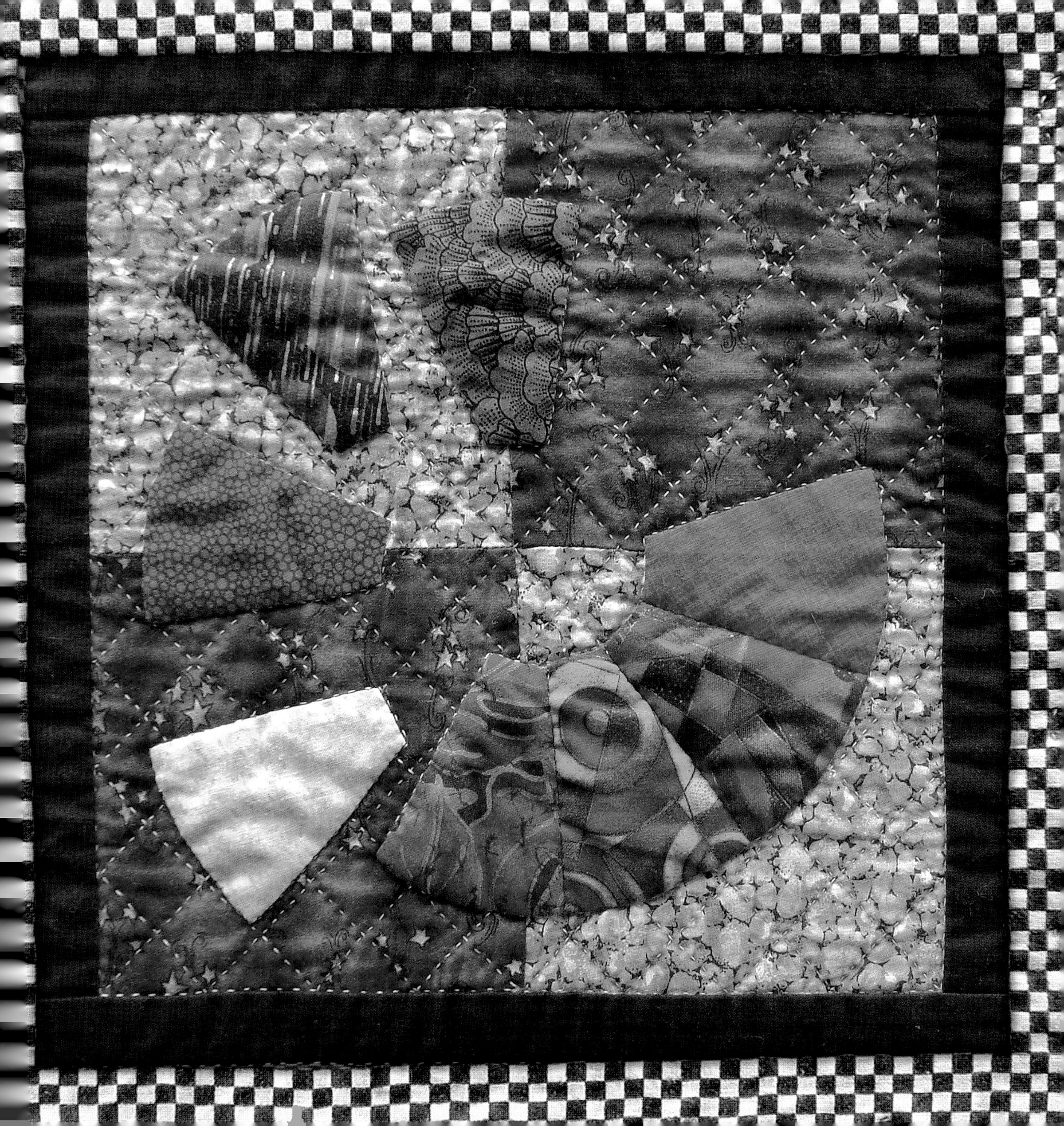

They all started searching for the china. "Where is your seam ripper?" Hanna asked the Repairwoman.

The Repairwoman found the seam ripper and together they picked out the china pieces. The Partner collected all the pieces into her scarf. Suddenly she knew where her style would come from — the pieces of antique china. *Can I put them in my hair?* she wondered. *Do I dare?*

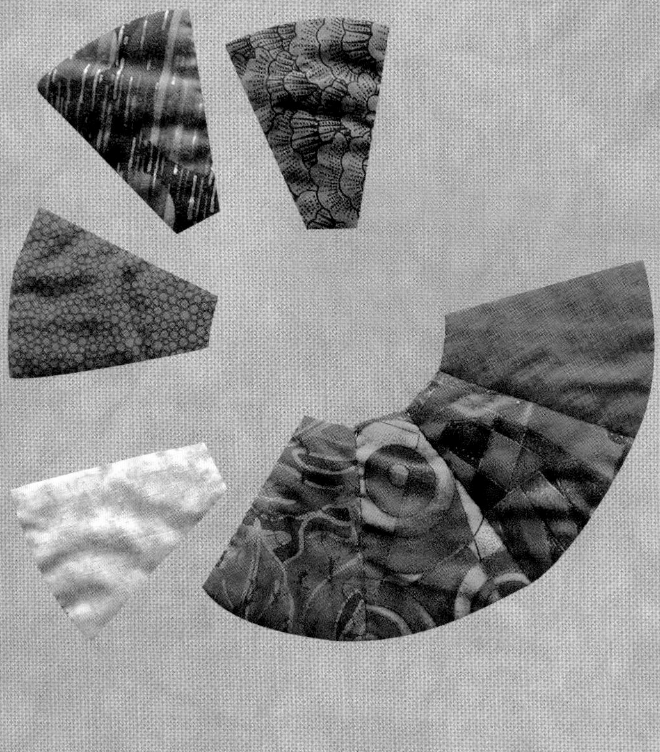

Chapter 12

The End

The troupe finally made it back to the crossroads. "Paducah, Paducah," called Hanna. "Where are you?"

Paducah, looking more like a judge than ever, approached the group with a critique sheet in her hand. "Well, Hanna, you're back. Now you must enter your quilt design in the show."

Hanna's heart sank. "But it's not quilted," she protested. "It will never be done in time."

"We'll keep you company, Hanna," said the Bear. "We can form a Quilting Bee." No one was more surprised by the Bear's words than the Bear herself. *Why didn't I think of this before? I can start a Bee. I don't have to find one.*

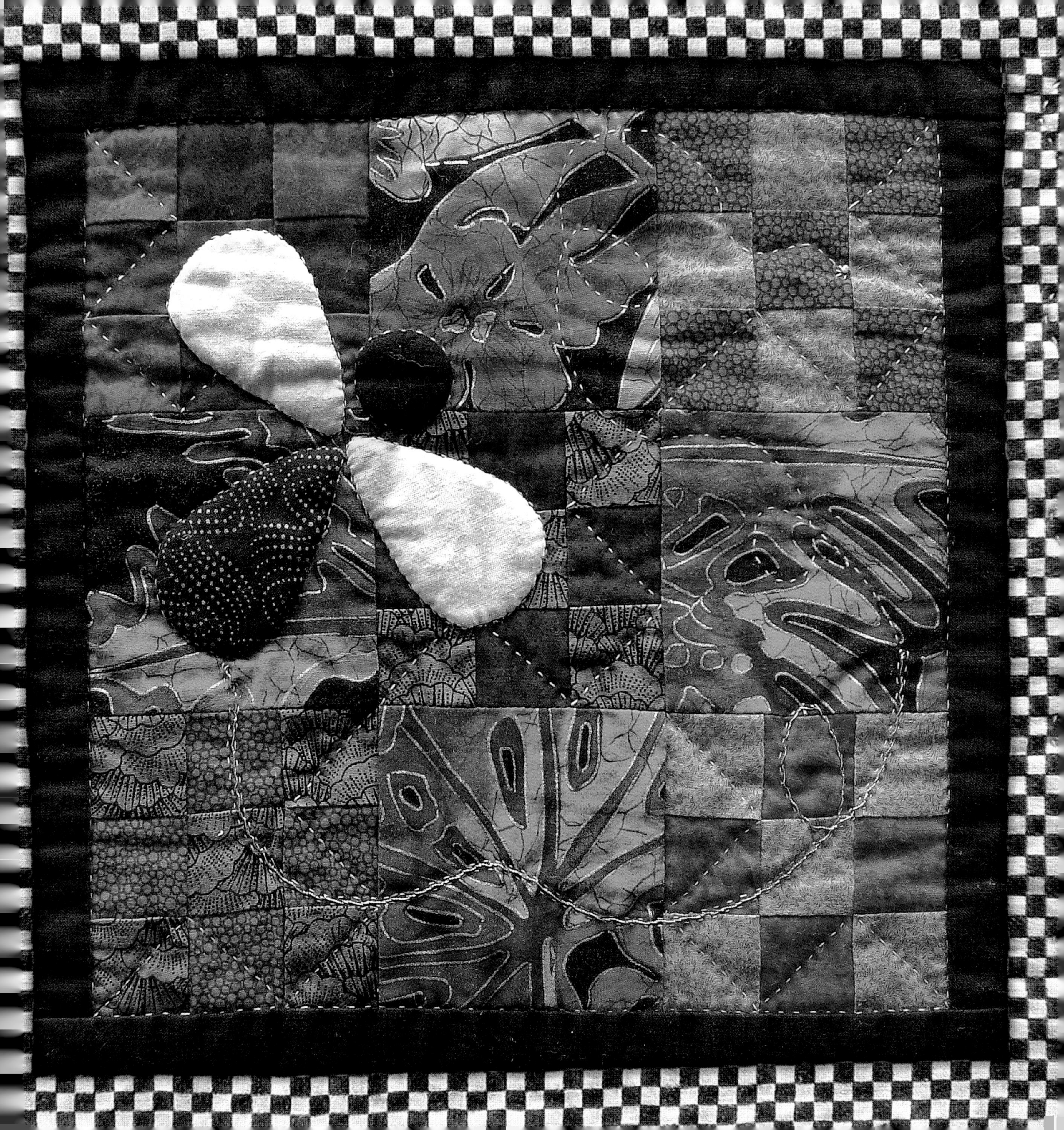

"Thank you, Bear. You are a wonderful friend, but I still don't know if I can get it done in time."

No one knew what to say, and everything seemed quiet and still. Then Hanna heard a voice. It was the Good Fairy Gadget whispering. "Just use the Ruby Thimble and rock the silver needle. You'll be done in no time. You always had inspiration inside of you. Now use it."

Hanna blinked, rubbed her eyes, and threw off the quilt.

"Aunt Hattie? Where are you? I had the most marvelous dream!"

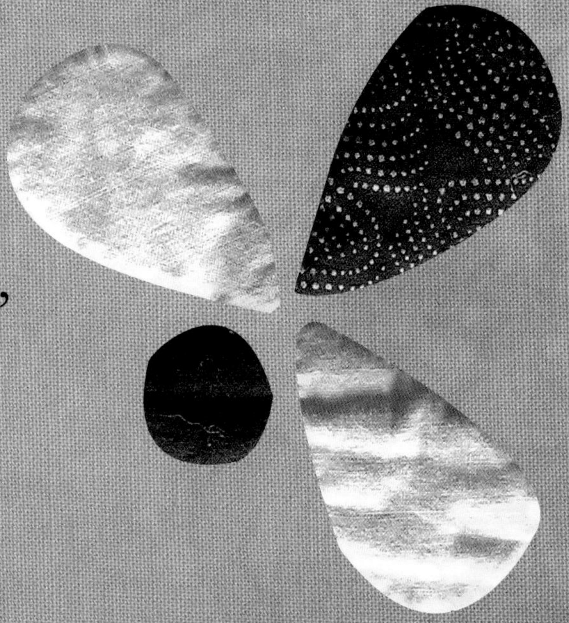

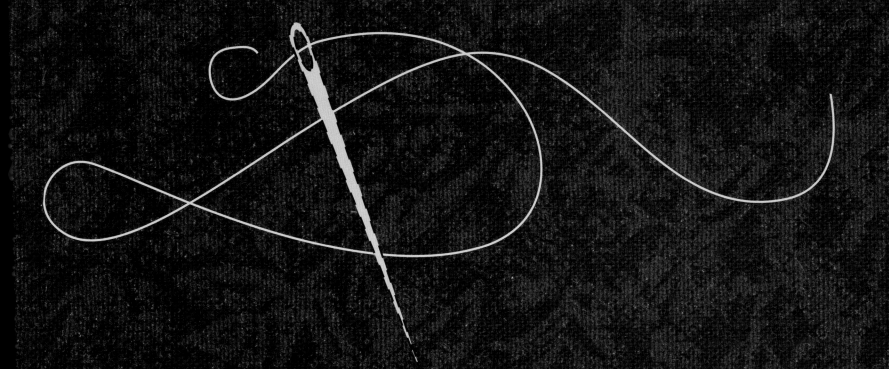

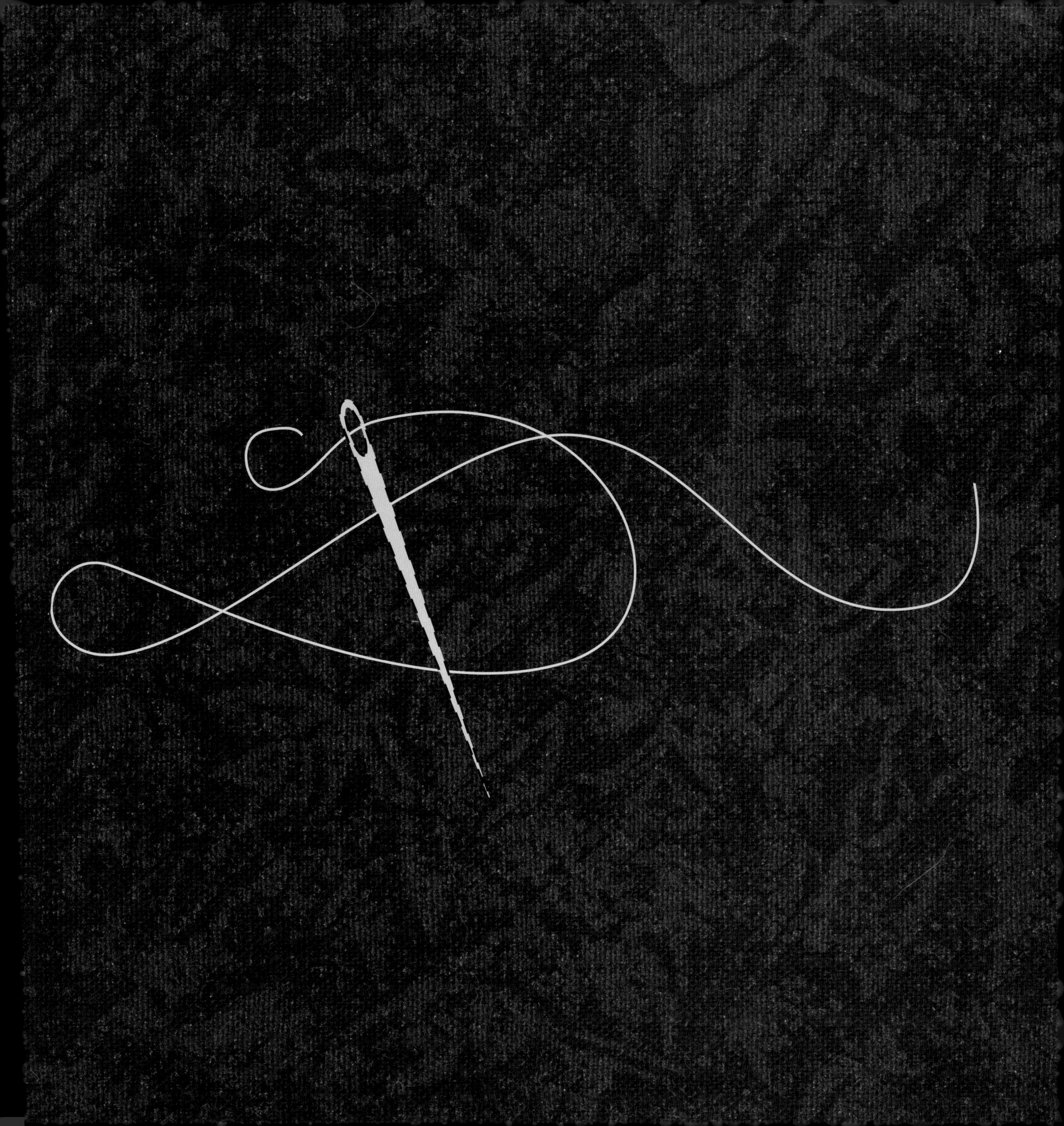

The Glossary

batik — A fabric-printing method in which white fabric is coated with a design block dipped in wax (the parts not to be dyed) and then the entire fabric is covered with dye. The wax is later removed to reveal the original design.

batting — Layers or sheets of cotton or wool or synthetic fibers used between the quilt top and backing. This is the middle layer and in general helps to provide warmth.

bobbin — A cylinder made of plastic or metal on which thread is wound. This is where the thread comes from that forms the underside of machine stitching.

featherweight — A portable sewing machine introduced by Singer Company at Chicago's 1933 World Fair. It is the most popular machine made by Singer, weighing only eleven pounds.

gadget — A small mechanical device with a practical use but often thought of as something you could do without.

inspiration — The act of influencing, suggesting opinions, or launching ideas.

Paducah — A city in western Kentucky near the Ohio River; population 27,256; the location of the Museum of the American Quilter's Society.

partner — One of two or more persons who play or work together.

stiletto — A pointed instrument for piercing holes or guiding fabric toward the needle while machine sewing.

style — A distinctive manner of expression in clothing or speech or behavior.

thimble — A pitted cap or cover made of metal that is worn on the finger to protect it from needle pricks while pushing the needle in hand sewing.

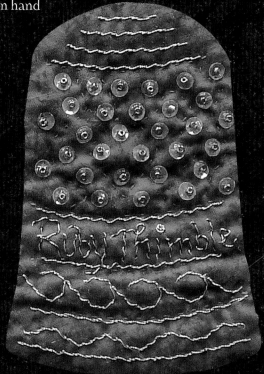

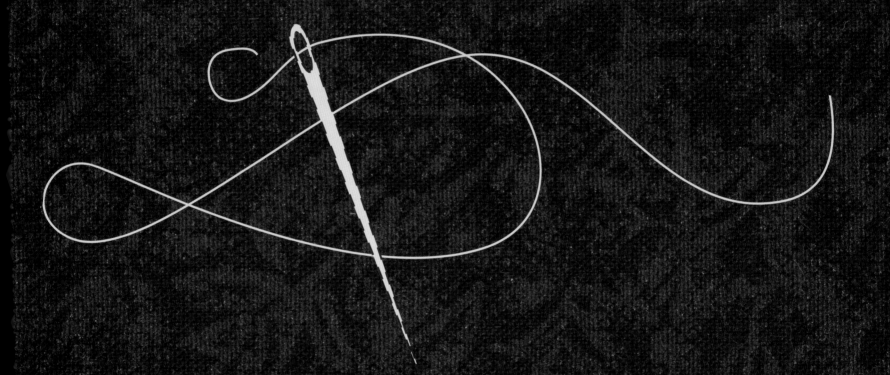

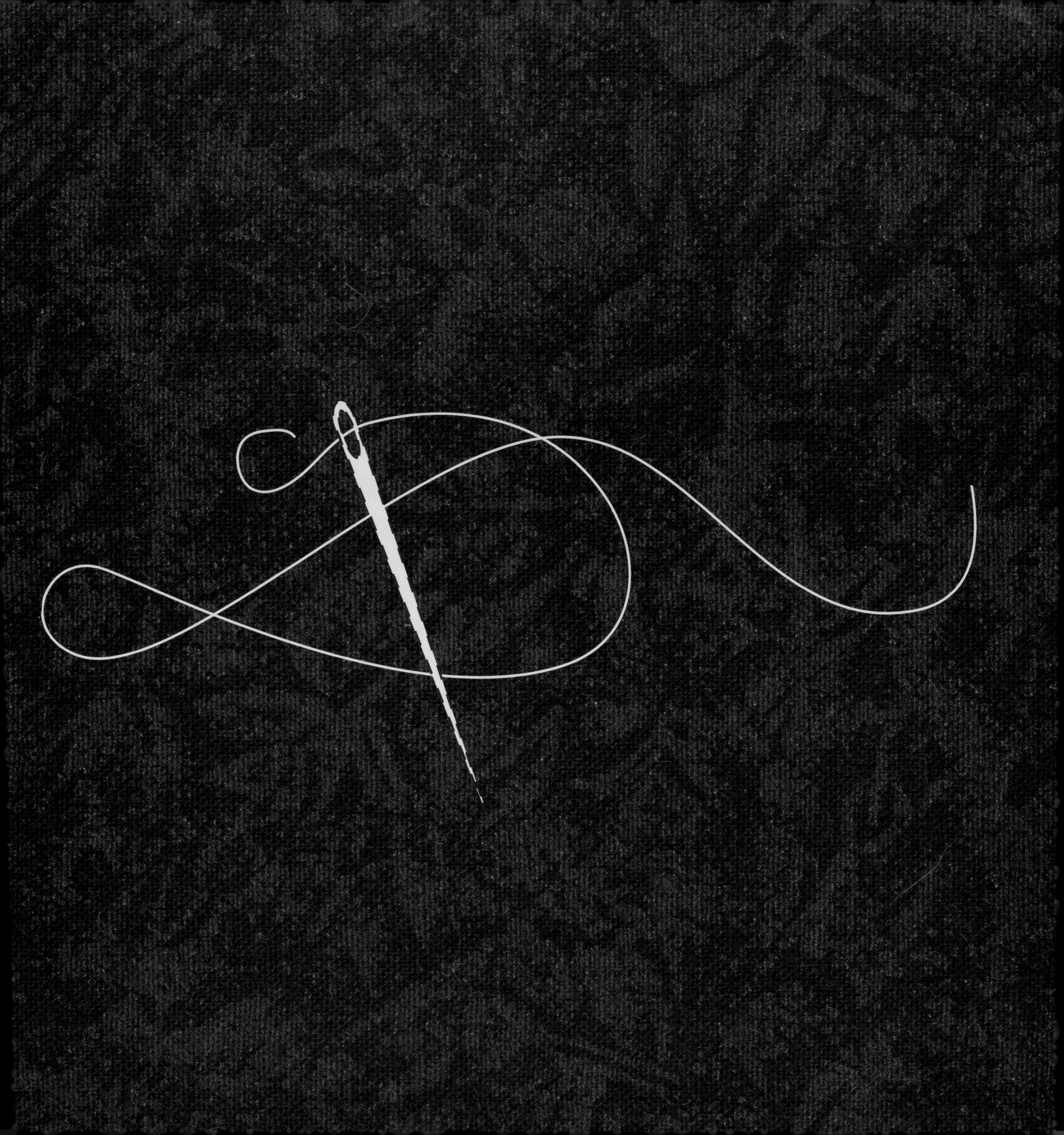

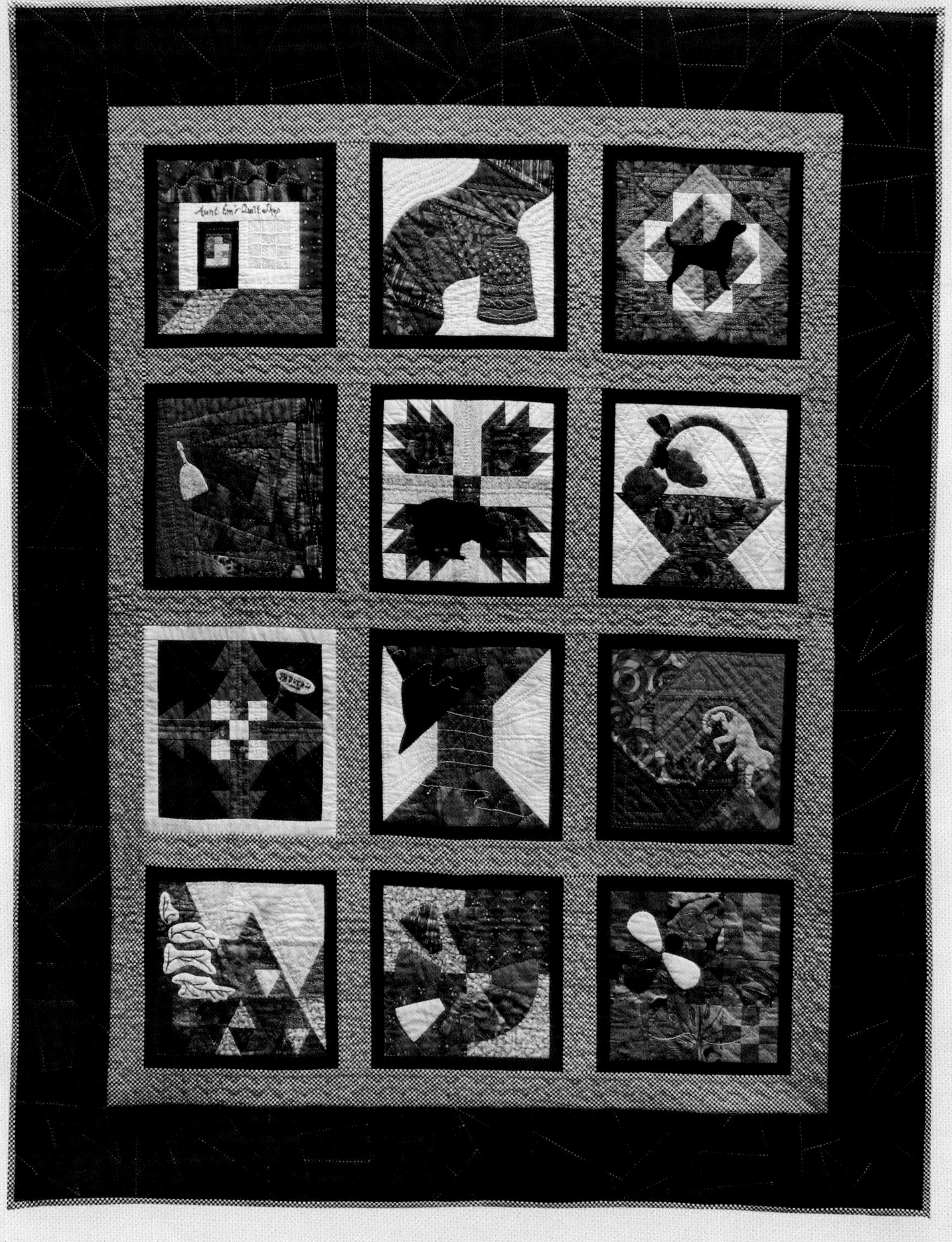
Aunt Em's Quilt Shop

***The Dream*, 49" x 61"**
Made by Gyleen X. Fitzgerald

Making
Your Very Own
Dream Story Quilt

And you thought you were done with *The Dream*. Not a chance. To complete your dream quilt you will need to go it alone (but I've added lots of help). I have provided some basic ideas, but the final decisions are all yours. Each block can be personalized by combining elements from other blocks, or you can choose to just complete the appliqué or just do the piecing. Try re-reading the story to get other ideas, like adding buttons in the sashing of the Witch's Block. When selecting fabric, you can match my selection or select an entirely different colour palette.

If you have not attempted a quilt before, don't feel overwhelmed. I have provided some excellent resources that will teach you the basics.

Another alternative is to photo transfer the full block pattern to cloth and use permanent fabric pens to complete the blocks. Tying, machine quilting, or hand quilting are all acceptable ways to finish your masterpiece! Remember, this is *your* dream.

Supplies

- 21 Fat Quarters (22" x 18") in assorted colours. Select both large and small prints. You will need a few light prints and a lot of bright prints. Be bold and mix dots, plaids, stripes, and flowers.
- 2 yards for block border and quilt border
- 2 yards for sashing and binding
- 4 yards for the quilt backing
- 1 twin size batting
- 1 yard of extra-light fusible webbing for appliqué
- 2 sheets (8" x 10") of template material
- Assorted embroidery thread for embellishments
- Basic sewing supplies, including rotary cutting equipment

General Instructions

All seams are ¼" unless otherwise noted. The unfinished blocks are 9½", which includes seam allowances. Press the seams as you go. Directions for paper piecing can be found in the resource books. Remove all paper from the paper-pieced blocks last. The appliqué is fused; follow manufacturers' instructions. Finish appliqué edges by buttonhole stitch, either by hand or machine, or by machine zig-zag. For ideas on colour placement, revisit the blocks in the story. And by all means please remember, there is no crying in quilting. Have fun, laugh a lot, and enjoy the process. If you make a mistake, that's the perfect place to put the appliqué. Work on any block of your choice!

Block Assembly Instructions

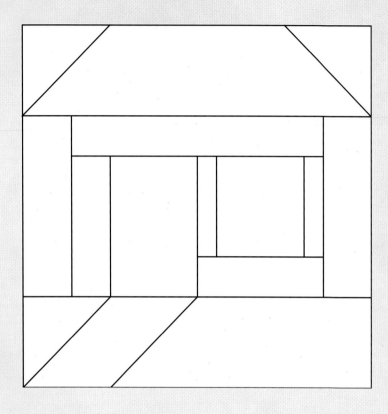

See full-size, mirrored, paper-piecing templates unit A and B on pages 72 – 73 and the quilt shop name embellishment on page 73.

Aunt Hattie's Quilt Shop

House blocks have been around since the beginning of quilting and no sampler would be complete without one. Paper piecing makes the construction quick and accurate.

- Copy both sections of the house pattern (including the seam allowances). Trim both units on the cutting line after the paper piecing is complete. Sew the units together to form the block, and then remove paper. Embellish the house front (piece #7) with the name of the quilt shop using a stem stitch and two strands of embroidery floss. Consider putting curtains in the window and a micro mini-quilt on the door.

Unit A

- #1 Cut 1 Window, 3" x 3".
- #2 & #3 Cut 2 House, 3" x 1".
- #4 Cut 1 House, 4" x 1½".
- #5 Cut 1 Door, 4" x 3".
- #6 Cut 1 House, 4" x 1½".
- #7 Cut 1 House, 7" x 1½".
- #8 & #9 Cut 2 Sky, 5" x 1¾".
- #10 Cut 1 Roof, 9½" x 3".
- #11 & #12 Cut 1 Sky, 3" square (cut in half on the diagonal).

Unit B

- #1 Cut 1 Grass, 3" x 7½".
- #2 Cut 1 Sidewalk, 3" x 5".
- #3 Cut 1 Grass, 4" square.

Ruby Thimble

Ruby Thimble is an original block that uses many techniques. The Fabric Road is paper pieced, then appliquéd to the background square. The thimble is appliquéd, then embellished.

- Copy the Fabric Road pattern (including seam allowances). Paper piece the road.

- Trim road on the cutting line after the paper piecing is complete.

- Remove paper and appliqué the road to the background fabric (at least 10½" square).

- Next appliqué the thimble, embellish.

- Last, trim the block to 9½".

See full-size, mirrored, paper-piecing template of Ruby Thimble on page 80.

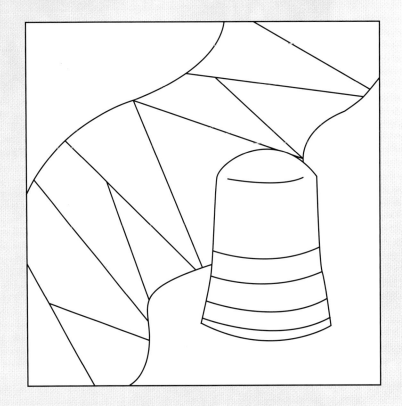

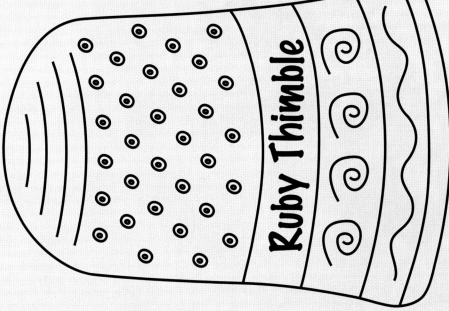

Full-size Ruby Thimble appliqué

Corn and Beans

The earliest dating of this block is 1895, and it's still going strong. Just changing the colour placement yields a completely different effect. Since this is your quilt, try placing the colours in various locations before sewing. Use at least 5 fabrics for this block, covering the range of dark, medium, medium-light, and light.

- Cut 20 squares, 2⅜"; cut each square in half on the diagonal for a total of 40 triangles.

- Cut 4 squares, 3⅞"; cut each square in half on the diagonal for a total of 8 triangles.

- To assemble, follow the sketch sequence, make 4. Sew the 4 sections together to form the block. Appliqué Bobbin the dog anywhere on the block.

See full-size, appliquéd dog template for Corn and Beans on page 74.

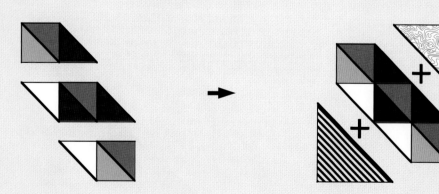

Sketch

Log Cabin

This is a traditional block with a free-spirited twist. Paper piecing is the most accurate method, or you can try the "sew and hack" approach. There are no rules.

- Go in rounds, starting in the center. Lights or one colour palette on one side and darks or another colour palette on the other.

- Trim the block to 9½".

- Appliqué the oil can.

See full-size, mirrored template of Log Cabin on page 79.

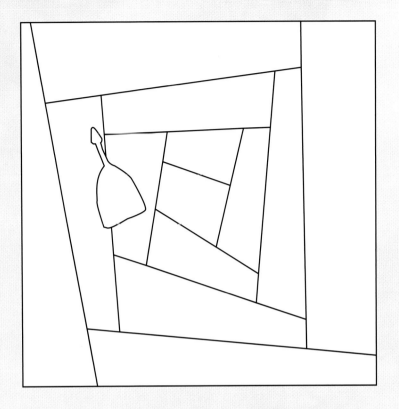

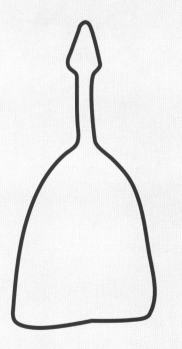

Full-size Log Cabin appliqué

61

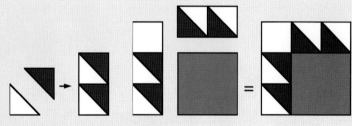

Sketch 1

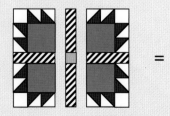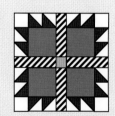

Sketch 2

Bear's Paw

If you struggled with Corn and Beans, this block will be a relief. It has been simplified by using a variation of the block (resulting in fewer nails). Possibly use 5 fabrics, but that may be a little too much. The nails and the footpad should be different.

For the paw

- Cut 8 squares, $2\frac{1}{8}$"; cut each square in half on the diagonal for a total of 16 triangles.
- Cut 4 squares, 3".

For the background

- Cut 8 squares, $2\frac{1}{8}$"; cut each square in half on the diagonal for a total of 16 triangles.
- Cut 4 squares, $1\frac{3}{4}$".

For the center cross

- Cut 4 rectangles, 2" x $4\frac{1}{4}$".
- Cut 1 square, 2".

- To assemble, follow the sketch 1 sequence, make 4.
- Sew the 4 sections to the center cross pieces to form the block per sketch 2.
- Appliqué the Bear anywhere on the block. A mismatched seam is a good place.

See full-size, appliquéd bear template for Bear's Claw on page 74.

Basket of Poppies

Basket of Poppies is an original design on a traditional theme. It is easier to build this block up in diagonal rows similar to the Corn and Beans block. Try selecting a medley of closely related fabrics to form the basket.

- Cut 10 triangles using template I.

- Cut 2 polygons for background using template II; cut 1 as a mirror image.

- Cut 1 background for block top, 5" x 9½".

- Cut 1 strip, ⅜" x 12" for basket handle.

- Start by sewing triangles into squares; make 3. Make diagonal rows to form the basket per sketch 1.

- Sew a triangle to the end of each polygon per sketch 2. Sew polygon assembly to each side of the basket. Using the completed block as your guide, appliqué the basket handle to background of block top. Sew basket assembly to block top. Appliqué the poppies and embroider the stems.

See full-size templates I and II for Basket of Poppies on page 78 and appliquéd poppy template on page 75.

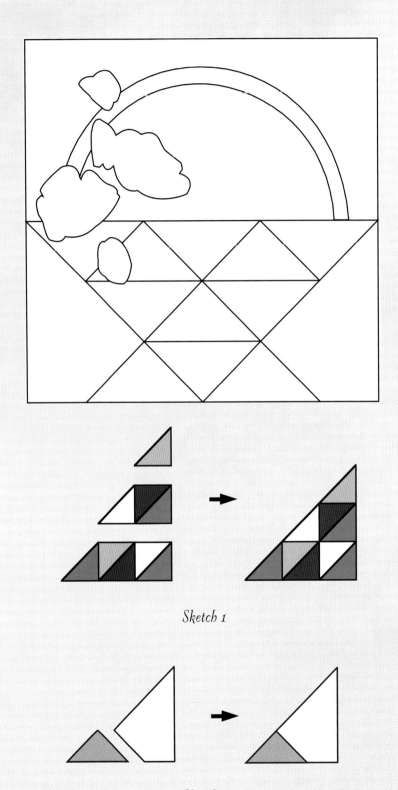

Sketch 1

Sketch 2

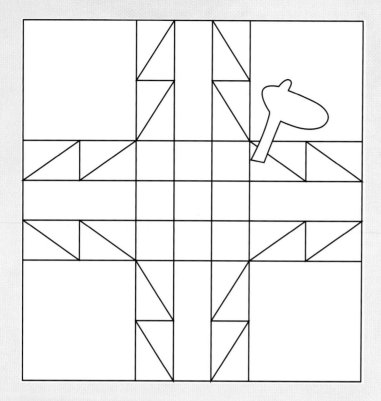

Sketch 1

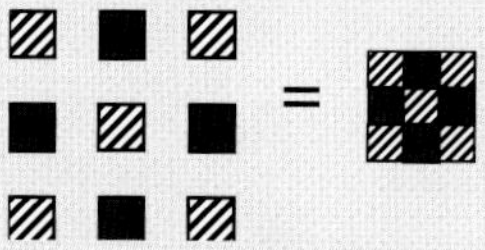

Paducah Crossroads

Paducah Crossroads is based on a nine-patch grid within a nine patch. The only tricky part is the elongated triangles. The paper-piecing templates for the triangles make this a snap. Just remember that they are orientated for left and right. The appliqué can go anywhere.

- Cut 4 squares, 3½".

- Cut 9 squares, 1½", using 2 fabrics.

- Cut 4 rectangles, 1½" x 3½".

- Cut 32 rectangles, 3" x 2" using 2 fabrics.

- Using the paper-piecing templates and the 3" x 2" rectangles, make 4 left and 4 right elongated triangle sections. Trim on the cutting line. Sew 2 elongated triangles to each long side of the 1½" x 3½" rectangles. Make 4. Sew 3½" squares to elongated triangle assembly. Make 2. See sketch 1.

- Using the (9) 1½" squares, sew 1 nine-patch block. See sketch 2. Sew 2 elongated triangle assemblies to each side of the nine-patch block.

- Complete the final assembly of the block per sketch 3. Remove paper when block is complete. Appliqué the sign for Paducah.

See full-size templates III and IV o8f Paducah Crossroads on page 78 and full-size, appliquéd Paducah sign template on page 75.

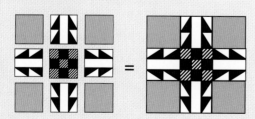

Sketch 2

Sketch 3

Spool Witch

Spool Witch is a simple traditional block. Just watch out for those mitered corners. To assemble the block, I suggest using my easy method; you will square up once the block is complete.

- Cut 4 strips, 4" x 10", using 2 different fabrics.

- Cut 1 square, 3½".

- Center 3½" square on rectangle. Sew across edge. Press toward the square. Repeat on the other side.

- Using your second fabric, center 3½" square on rectangle. Sew across edge. Press toward center. Repeat this on the other side.

- Looking at the WRONG side of the square, remove all stitches in the ¼" seam allowance area.

- Fold the square diagonally (with RIGHT side together) and match up outside edges of the rectangles on both ends of square. Mark the 45-degree line. Pin and sew on this line, taking care to stop at the exact corner of the square. Do this for the opposite corner. Trim off excess fabric beyond the sewing line, leaving ¼" seam allowance.

- Fold the square diagonally in the other direction and repeat the previous step. NOTE: The 45-degree line should be in line with the fold of the center.

- Square up to 9½".

- Appliqué the witch's hat in the corner on a diagonal. Embellish by putting golden thread on the hat and through the square.

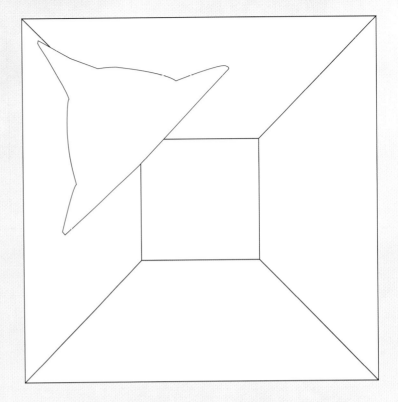

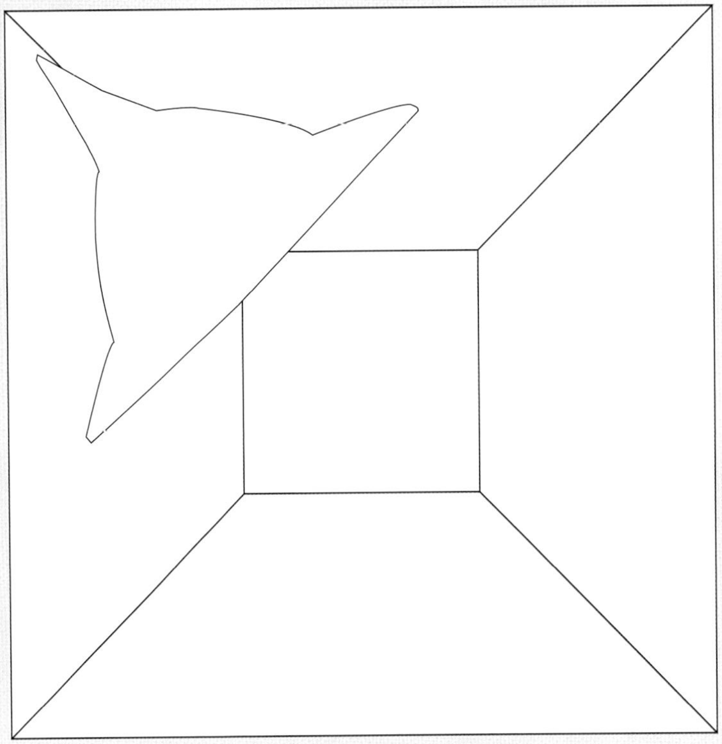

See full-size, appliquéd witch hat template for Spool Witch on page 76.

65

Monkey Wrench

Monkey Wrench is also known as a Snail's Trail. Paper piecing is the easiest method to construct this block accurately.

- To make the 4-patch center: cut 4 squares, $2\frac{1}{4}$", from 4 fabrics. Sew 2 squares together to form pairs, then sew 2 pairs together to form the 4-patch. See sketches 1 and 2.

- Match the lines on the paper-piecing template with the seams of the 4-patch. Pin into position.

- **Round 1**: Cut 1 square, $3\frac{1}{4}$", in each colour; 4 total.

- **Round 2**: Cut 1 square, $4\frac{1}{4}$", in each colour; 4 total.

- **Round 3**: Cut 1 square, $5\frac{1}{2}$", in each colour; 4 total.

- Cut the squares in half on the diagonal for triangles. You will have one unused triangle in each size and colour.

- Colour placement of the triangles must align with the corresponding colour on the 4-patch. Begin paper piecing by adding triangles in rounds counterclockwise. The first triangle is the same colour of the top 4-patch square. Place the first triangle on the top left side of the paper-piecing template. The colours must be sewn in order of the 4-patch. If you do not put the colours on in order, the block will not spin — but it will be creative.

- Trim on the cutting line ($9\frac{1}{2}$") and remove paper. Appliqué the monkey climbing down if you wish.

See full-size template for Monkey Wrench on page 81 and full-size, appliquéd monkey template on page 76.

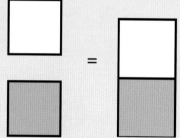

Sketch 1

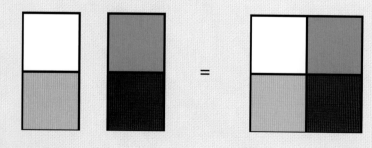

Sketch 2

Batting Tree

An original free-form block made from pyramids instead of triangles. You can decide how many colours and fabrics to use and where to place them.

- Begin by cutting an assortment of pyramids and moving them about until you are pleased with the quilt block layout like the one to the right.

- Cut 32 small pyramids using template V.

- Cut 13 large pyramids using template VI.

- Assemble 8 small pyramids in units of four as shown in sketch 1.

- Following the layout of sketch 2, sew units to large pyramids to form rows. Sew row to row to complete the block. The end of the rows will be jagged and will require sizing to 9½".

- Appliqué the tree along the edge of the block.

See full-size templates V and VI for Batting Tree on page 78 and full-size, appliquéd tree template on page 77.

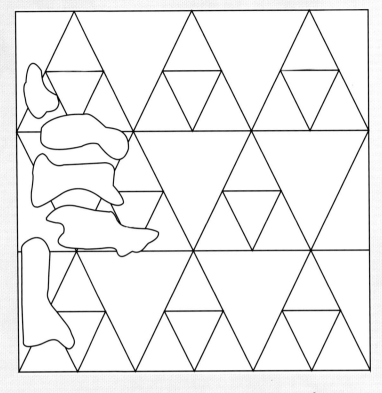

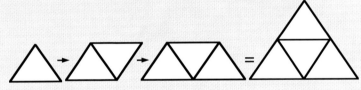

Sketch 1

Row 1

Row 2

Row 3

Sketch 2

67

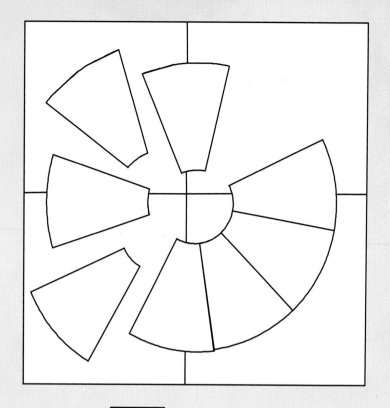

Broken China

Broken China is a combination of a 4-patch block and Baby Ester. I used a medley of fabrics to represent the pieces of broken china.

- To make the 4-patch background: Cut 4 squares, 5", from 2 fabrics. Sew 2 squares together to form pairs, then sew 2 pairs together to form the 4-patch. See sketches 1 and 2.

- Appliqué 8 wedges to the pieced background as shown in the completed block.

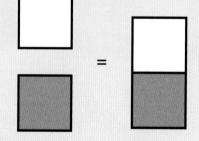

Sketch 1

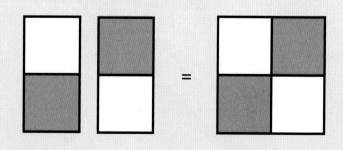

Sketch 2

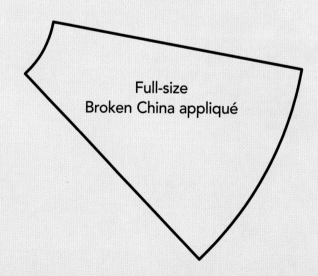

Full-size
Broken China appliqué

Quilting Bee

Quilting Bee is an original combination of two simple concepts: double nine-patch and honey-bee block.

- Cut 40 squares, 1½", from a variety of fabric. Make 5 small nine patches as shown in sketch 1.

- Cut 4 squares, 3½"; select a very large print.

- Alternate the squares with the nine-patches to form a bigger nine-patch block (hence the name double nine-patch) as shown in sketch 2.

- Appliqué the bee wings, head, and body. Embellish to get the air path. You're done!

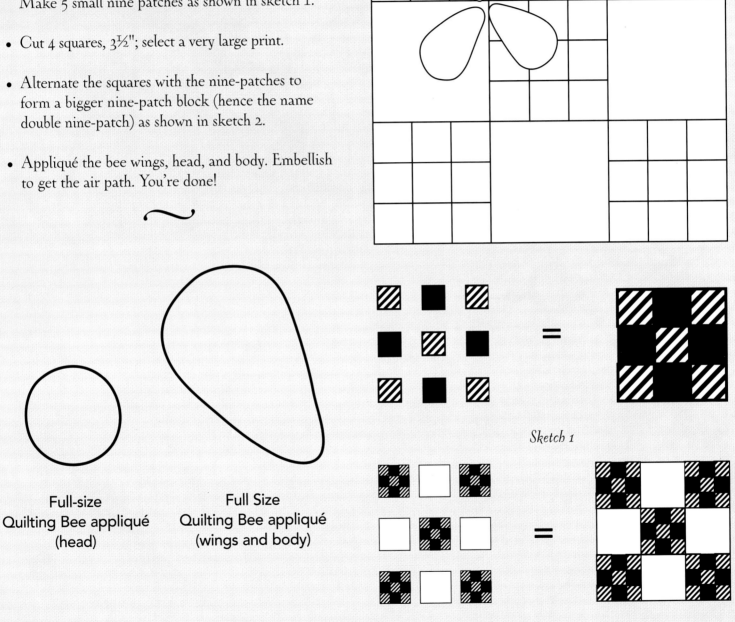

Full-size Quilting Bee appliqué (head)

Full Size Quilting Bee appliqué (wings and body)

Sketch 1

Sketch 2

Quilt Assembly

From the 2 yards of block border and quilt border fabric

- Cut 12 strips, 1½" x 42", for block border.
- Cut 8 strips, 4½" x 42", for quilt border.

From the 2 yards for sashing and binding fabric

- Cut 18 strips, 2½" x 42", for both sashing and binding.

For the block border, using the (12) 1½" strips

- Cut 48 strips, 12". Sew to each side of block. Trim even with the block. Sew strips to the top and bottom of the block. Repeat for all 12 blocks. Press seams toward border. Measure all blocks and size them to the smallest block. Remember to keep the block in the center as you cut.

For the sashing, using the (12) 2½" strips

- Measure block (including its border) from top to bottom; crosscut strips to this length. You will need 8 pieces; stitch to the sides of the block to form rows. Make 4 rows. Press seams toward sashing.

- Measure the length of each row (use average if this dimension is not the same). Crosscut 5 strips to this length and stitch between the rows; to the top of the first row; and to the bottom of the last row. Press seams toward sashing.

- Measure the length of the quilt from top to bottom; crosscut 2 strips to this length. You may need to connect some of the strips to get to this length. Stitch to the sides of the quilt.

For the quilt border, using the (8) 4½" strips

- Measure quilt from top to bottom; crosscut 2 strips to this length and stitch to the sides of the quilt. You may need to connect some of the strips to get to this length. Press seams toward border.

- Measure quilt from side to side; crosscut 2 strips to this length and stitch to top and bottom of quilt. Press seams toward border.

Finishing Flourishes

- Layer backing, batting, and quilt top. Baste layers together. Quilt as desired. The Dream was hand quilted with white cotton quilting thread. It contains a zig-zag pattern in the sashing and quilting outline in the border. Please feel free to finish yours using a sewing machine. The point is to get it finished so you can enjoy your art!

- Make binding by connecting the (6) 2½" strips. Fold and press in half lengthwise for a double-fold binding. Sew binding to quilt.

- Make a label to identify this quilt as your art; add a hanging sleeve and enjoy.

Jane Johnston's Dream Quilt

This is the story of Jane's quilt:

As Hanna makes her way from Aunt Hattie's Quilt Shop to the quilting bee, her topsy-turvy journey encounters many quilting challenges. She solves these with raw-edge piecing, thread sketching, and free-motion quilting. A novice to the rules of proper piecing, her points may not match, but the beaded embellishments and charms more than entice the eye. Her border is embellished with her "star" quilting partners sporting handmade polymer clay faces and frazzled lady hair; all are in a frenzy to get to that bee!

Jane's Dream Quilt, 44" x 56"
Made by Jane Johnston, an eclectic polymer
clay and quilt artist from Maryland.
She has her own style.

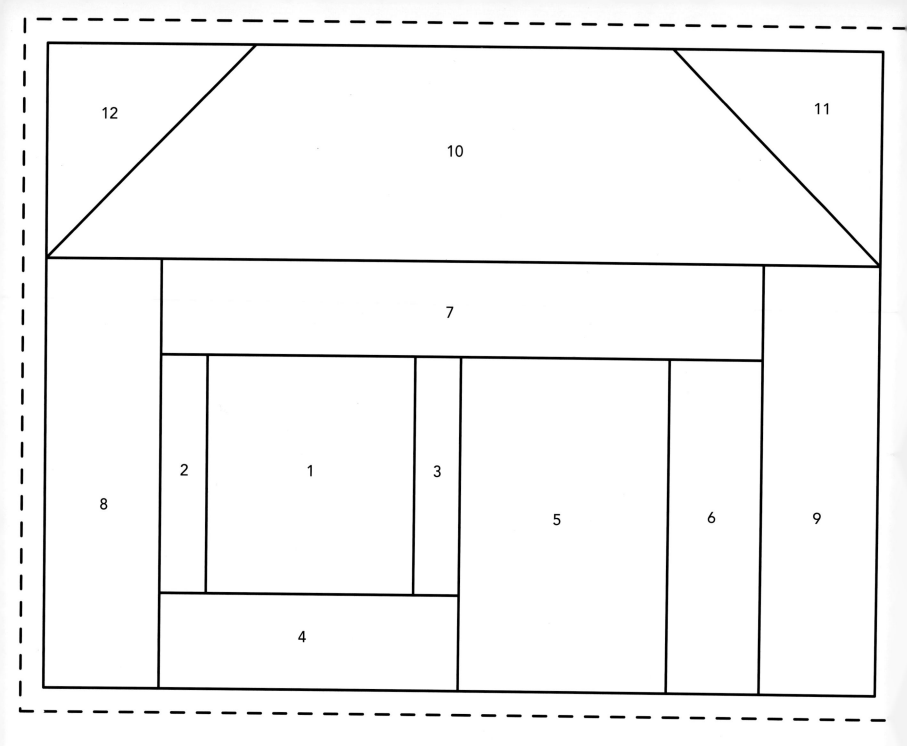

Aunt Hattie's Quilt Shop template, unit A. See page 73 for unit B and quilt shop name embellishment.

Aunt Hattie's Quilt Shop

Quilt shop name embellishment

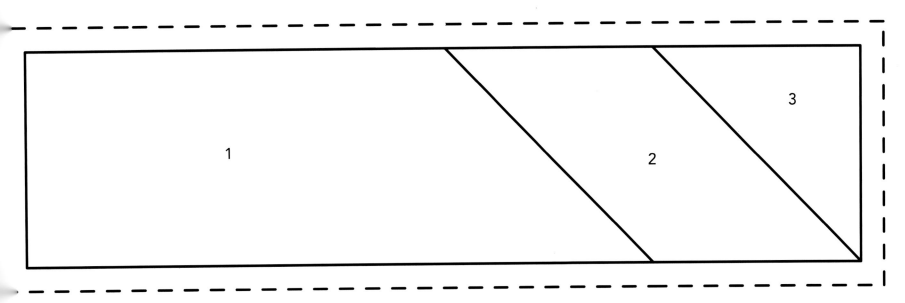

Aunt Hattie's Quilt Shop template, unit B. See page 72 for unit A.

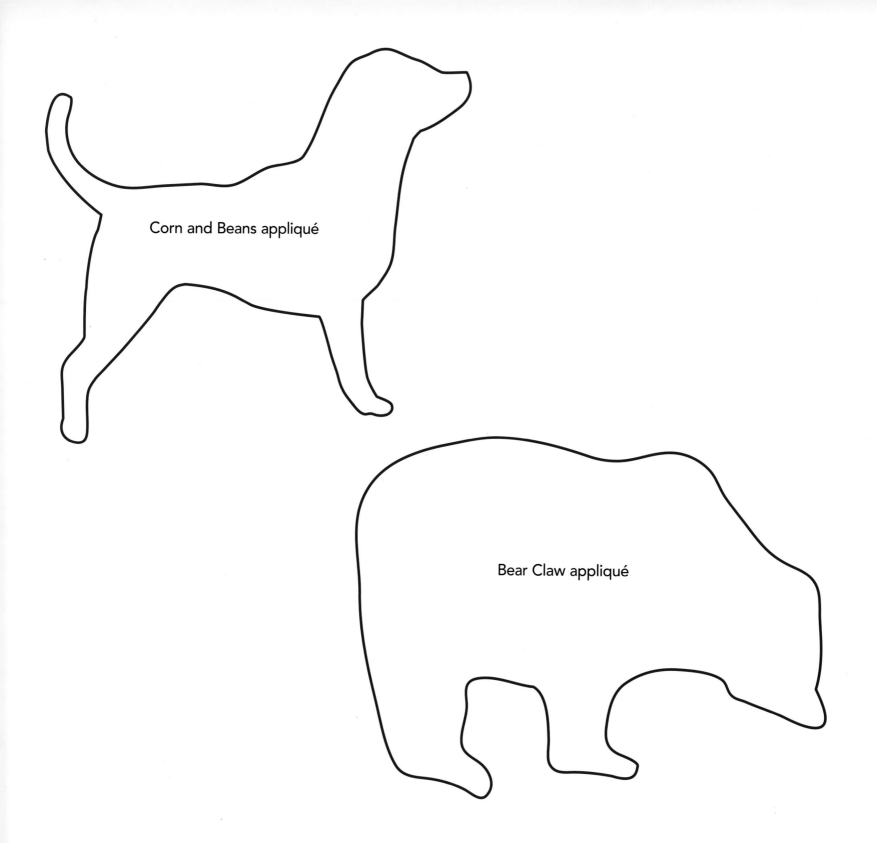

Corn and Beans appliqué

Bear Claw appliqué

74

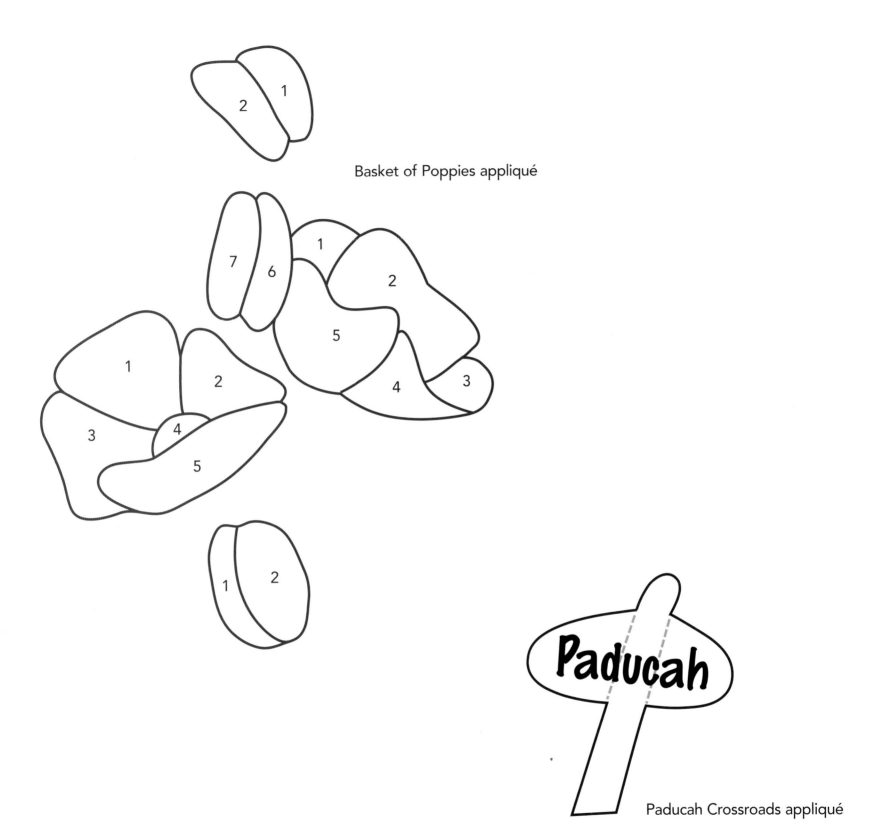

Basket of Poppies appliqué

Paducah Crossroads appliqué

75

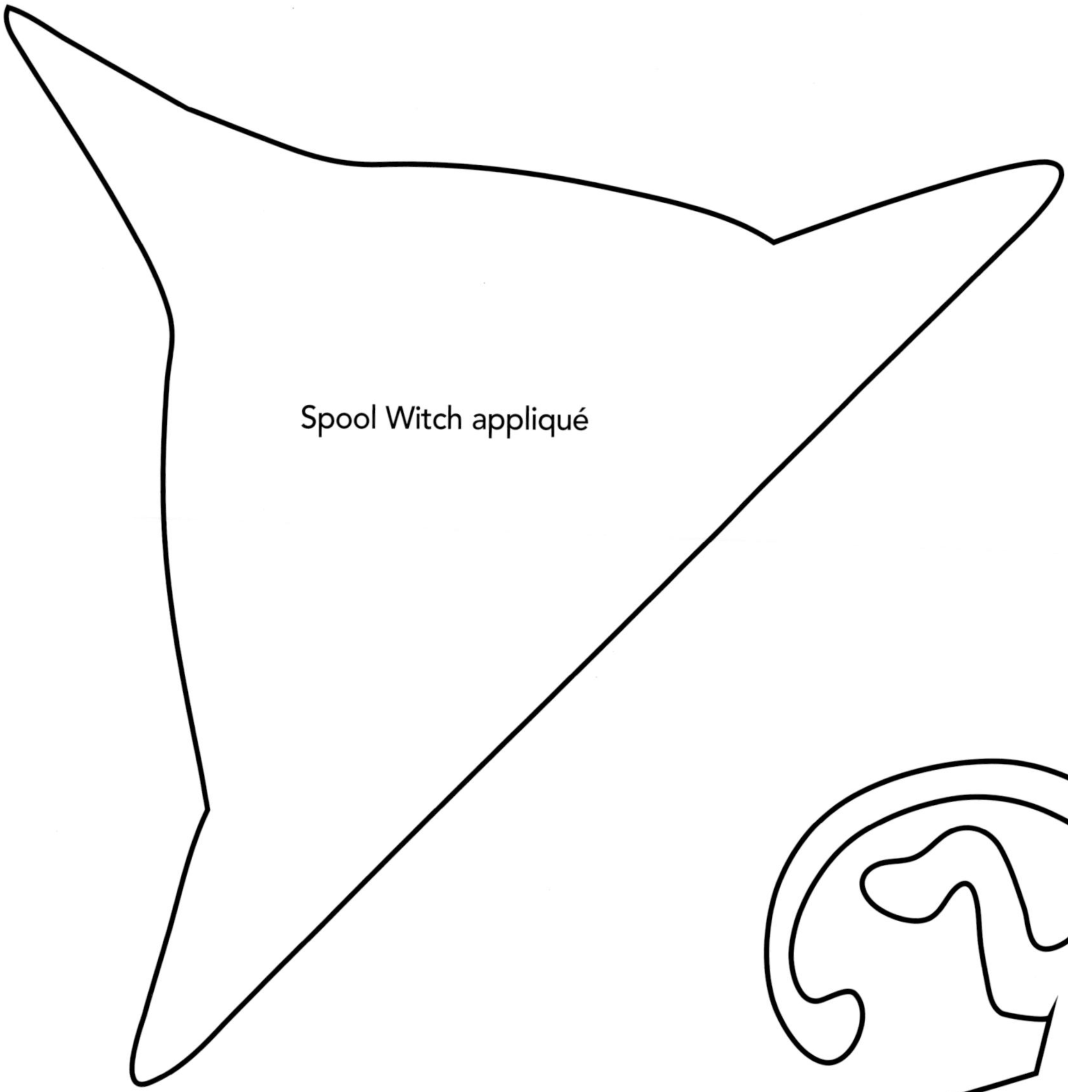
Spool Witch appliqué

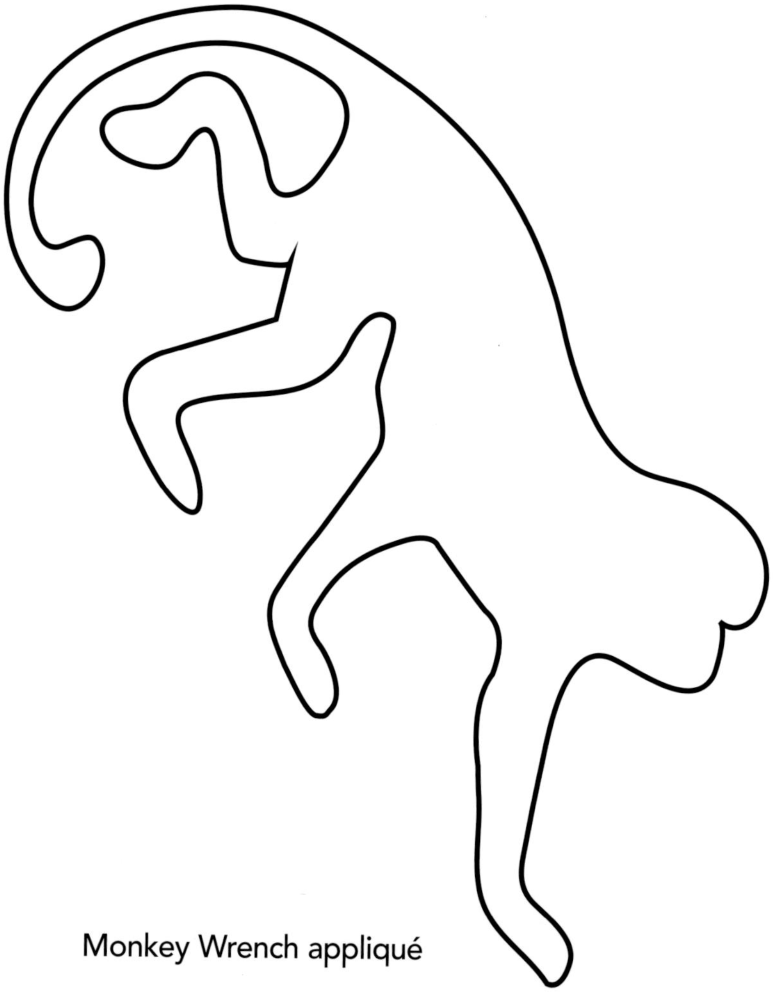

Monkey Wrench appliqué

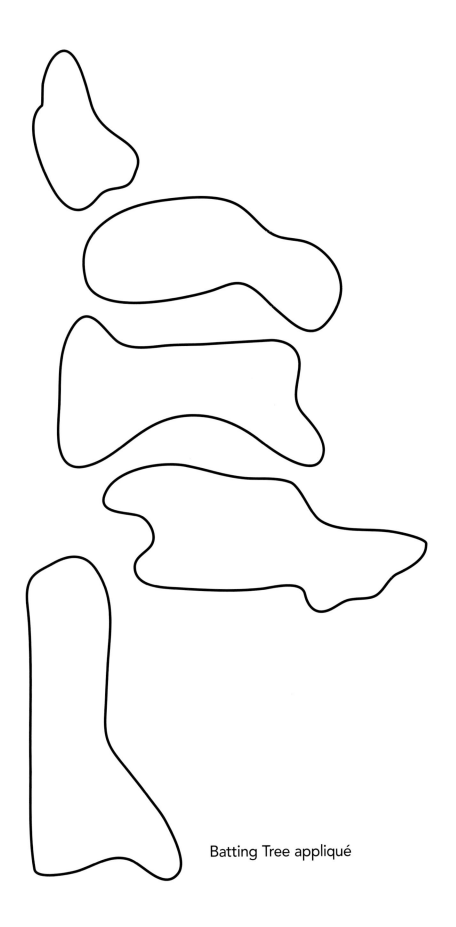

Batting Tree appliqué

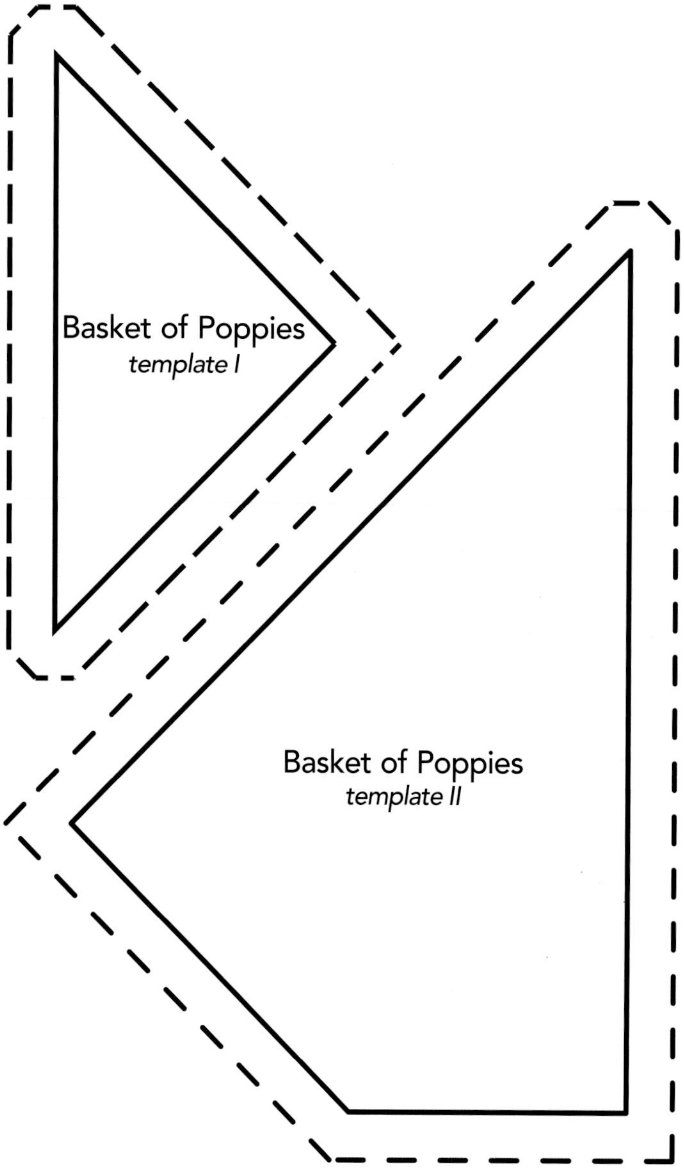
Basket of Poppies
template I
Basket of Poppies
template II

Paducah Crossroads

template III & IV

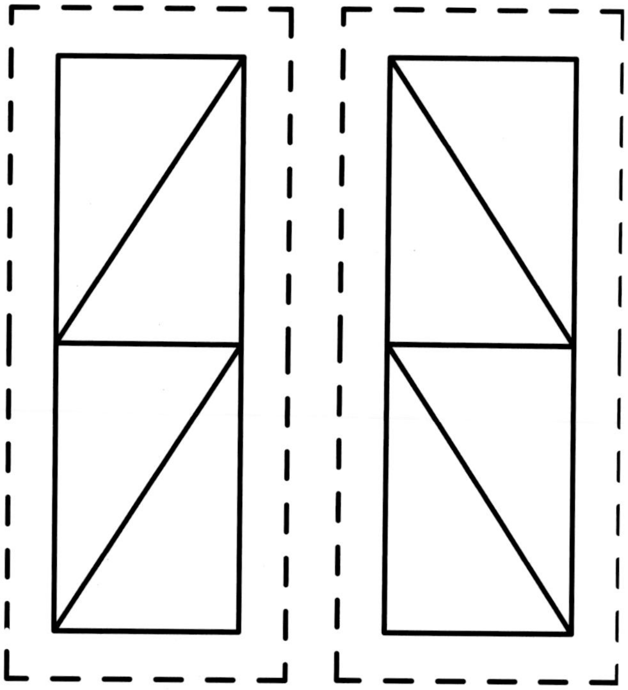

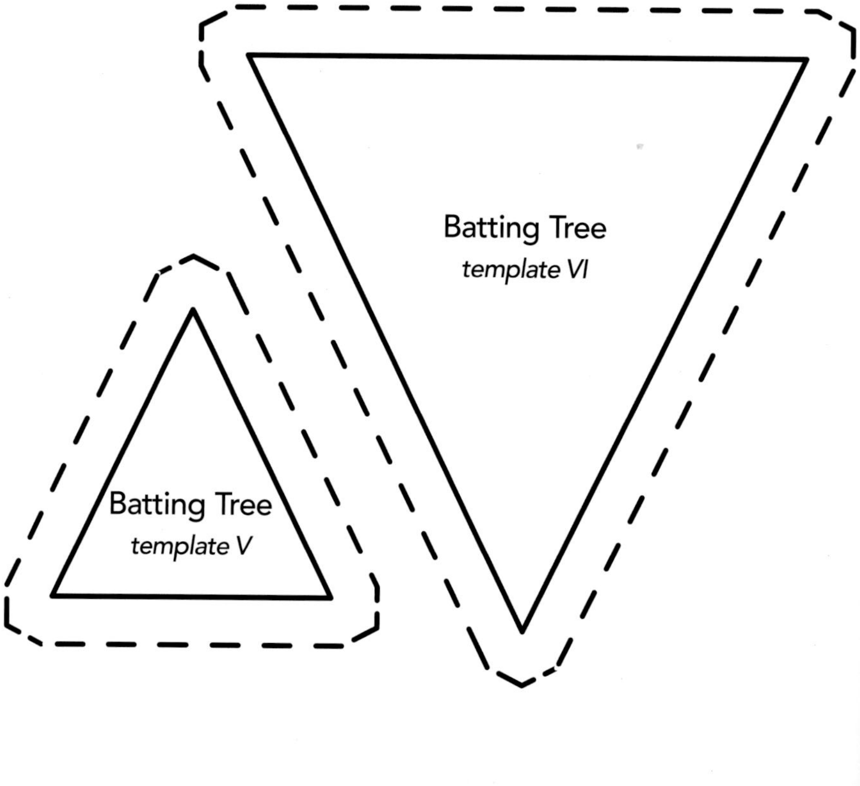
Batting Tree
template VI
Batting Tree
template V

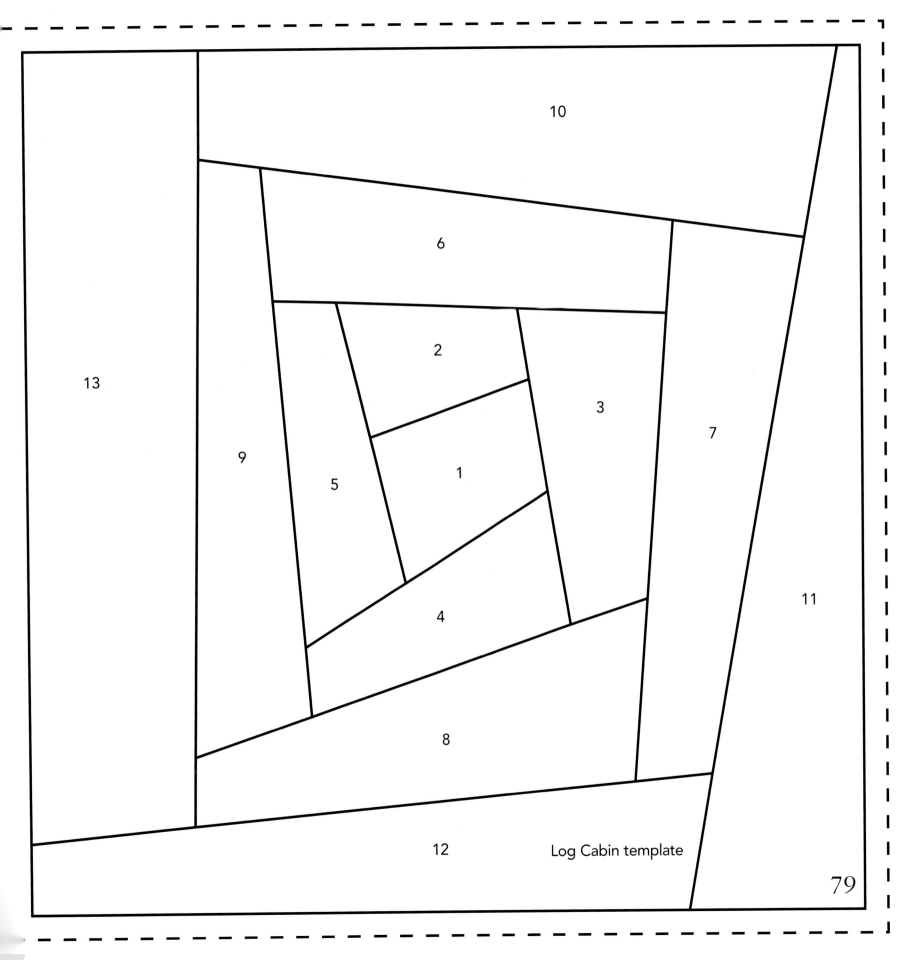

Log Cabin template

79

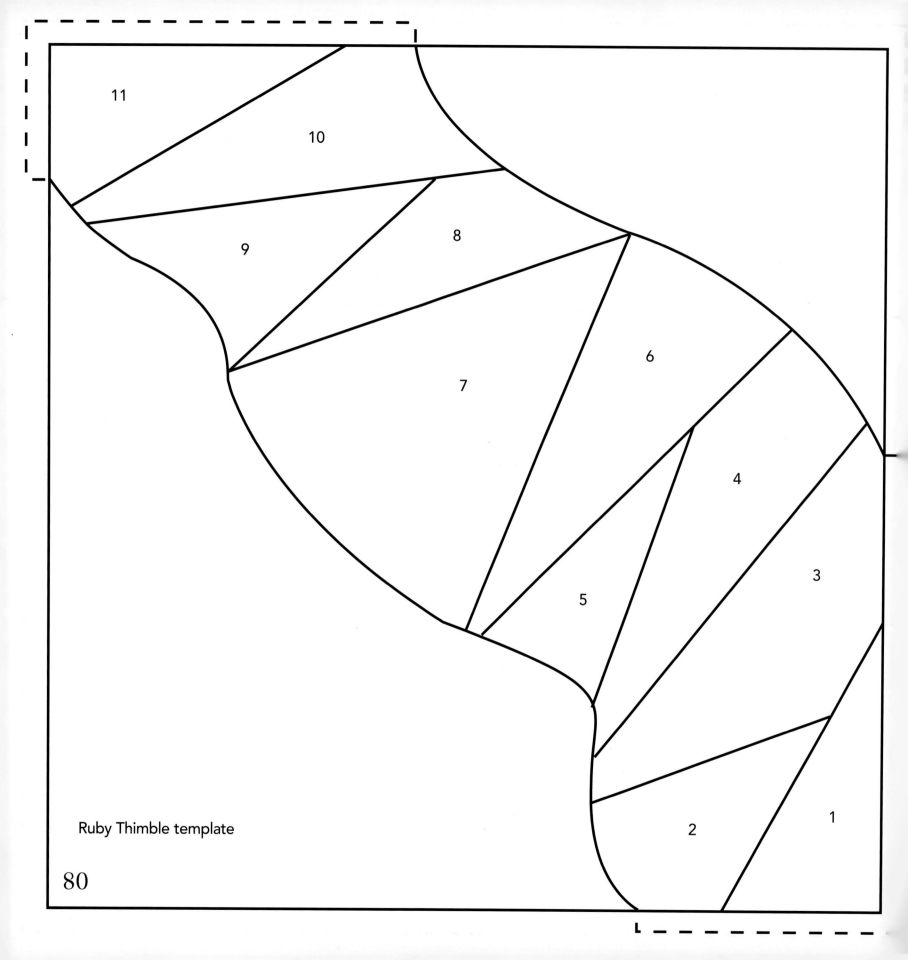

Ruby Thimble template

80

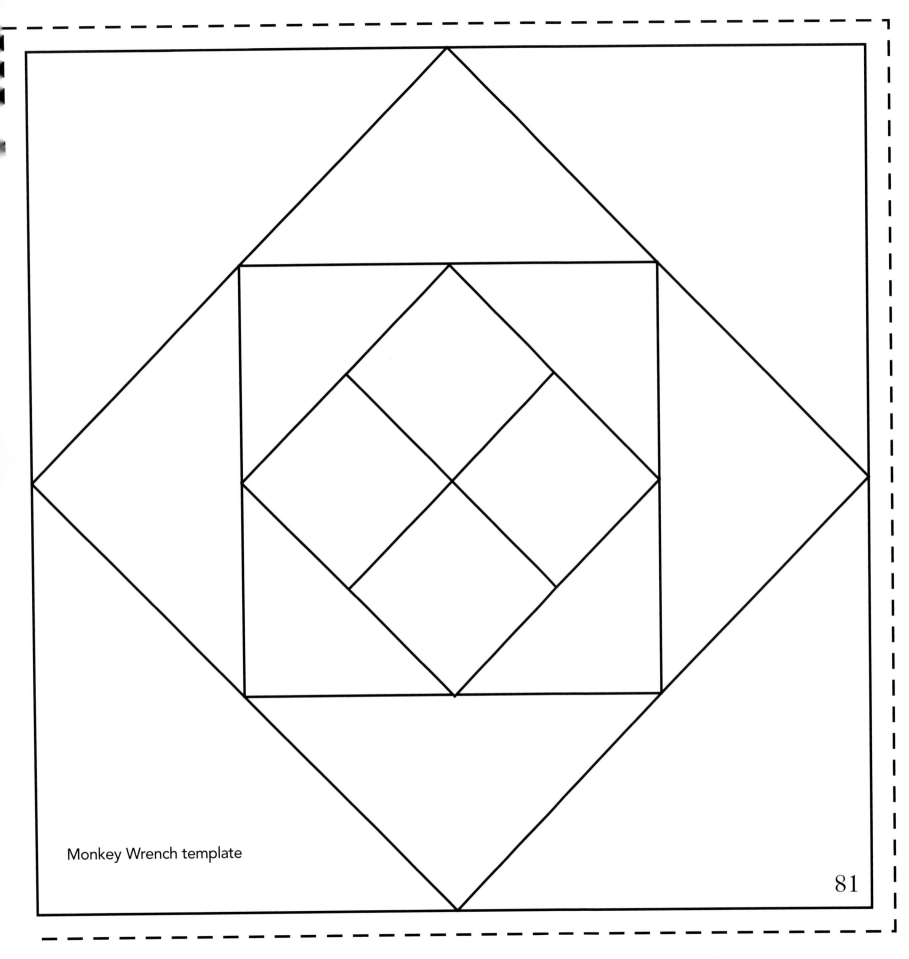

Monkey Wrench template

81

The Appendix

Resources

Don't neglect your local quilt shop as a source for fabric, notions, and classes. They will gladly answer quilting questions to help you complete your Dream quilt. A reasonable second choice is to use the resources listed here.

Quilting Supplies

Connecting Threads
PO Box 879760
Vancouver, WA 98687-7760
www.ConnectingThreads.com

Keepsake Quilting
Route 25B
PO Box 1618
Center Harbor, NH 03226-1618
www.keepsakequilting.com

Hancock's of Paducah
3841 Hinkleville Road
Paducah, KY 42001
800-845-8723
www.Hancocks-Paducah.com

Magazine

QUILT Magazine
800 Kennesaw Ave #220
Marietta, GA 30060
770-421-8160

Books

Color and Cloth: The Quiltmaker's Ultimate Workbook
by Mary Coyne Penders
The Quilt Digest Press
ISBN: 0-913327-20-4

Jenny Beyer's Color Confidence for Quilters
by Jenny Beyer
The Quilt Digest Press
ISBN: 0-913327-39-5

The Quilter's Ultimate Visual Guide
Rodale Press, Inc
ISBN: 0-87596-987-9

Quilter's Complete Guide
Marianne Fons and Liz Porter
Oxmoor House, Inc and Leisure Arts, Inc
ISBN: 0-8487-1152-1

Hand Dyed Fabric

Colourful Stitches
PO Box 247
Havre de Grace, MD 21078
410-459-9087
www.ColourfulStitches.com

Cherrywood Fabrics
PO Box 486
Brainerd, MN 56401
888-296-0967
www.CherrywoodFabrics.com

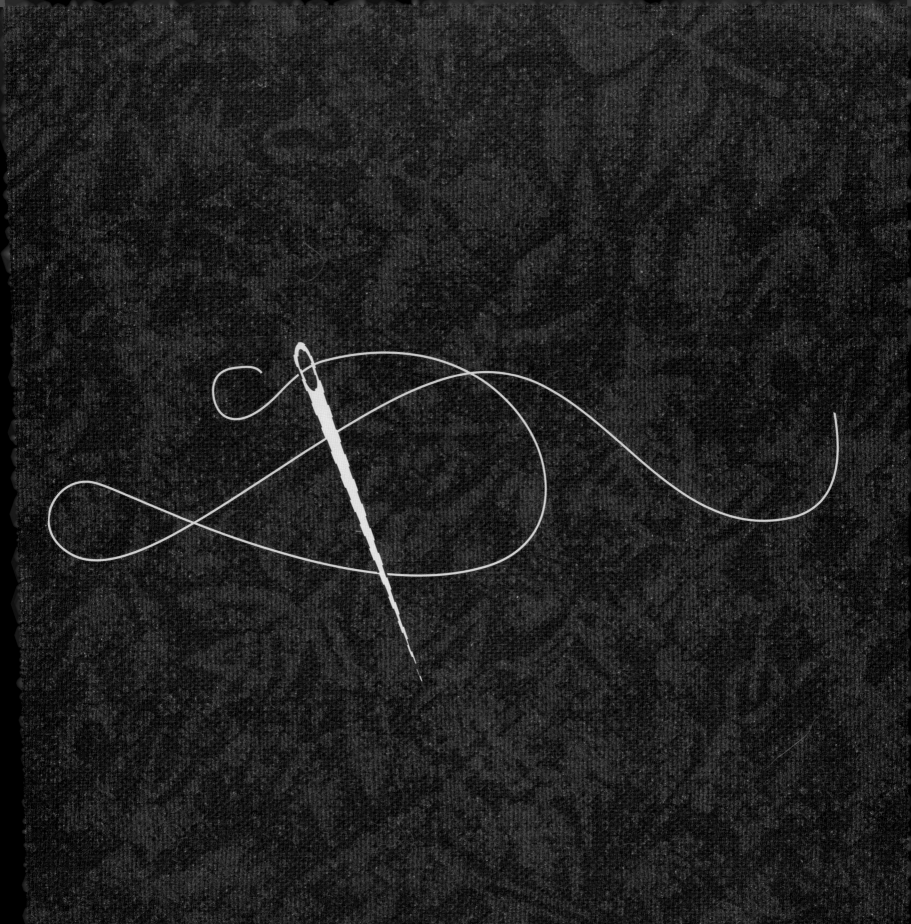

About the Author

Gyleen X. Fitzgerald attended a quilting workshop at a local store in 1981 and she's been quilting ever since. Her blend of colour, pattern, and texture brings a contemporary essence to traditional quilting. Gyleen's quilting awards include best of show and numerous blue ribbons in both local and national competitions. Her quilts have been published in *Patchwork Quilting, Quick Quilts,* and *Quilt Almanac.* In 1998 Gyleen opened Colourful Stitches, through which she offers workshops and lectures and sells notecards as well as hand-dyed fabrics and silk scarves. Gyleen has taught for guilds in several states and she offers a six-hour workshop throughout the year. She says her Quilt of Life — living with her husband James and boxers in Maryland — is complete.

Also Available...

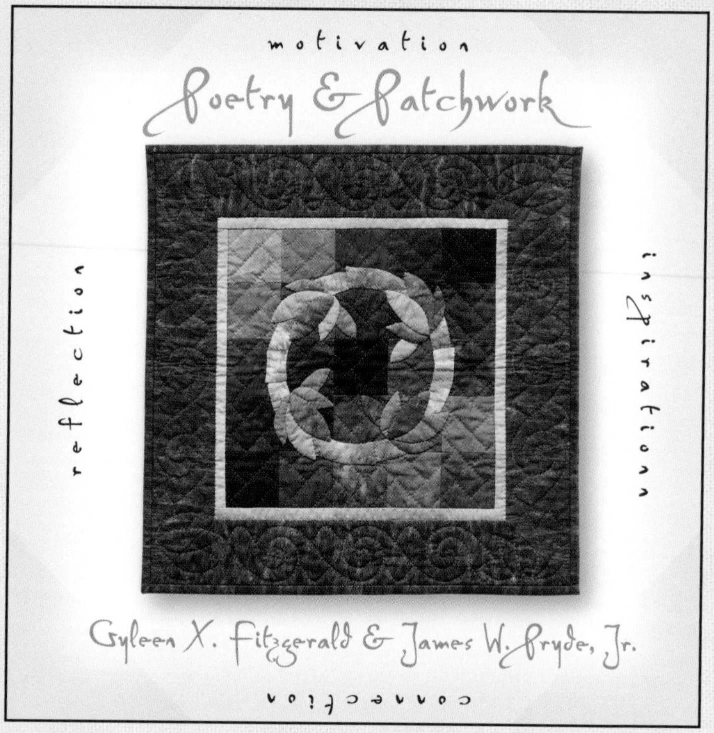
motivation
Poetry & Patchwork
reflection
inspiration
Gyleen X. Fitzgerald & James W. Pryde, Jr.
connection

Poetry and Patchwork
Price: $12.95
ISBN: 0-9768215-2-4

Lectures

Discover the art of colour blending, why some bed quilts work and others don't, or customize your own lecture! Visit www.ColourfulStitches.com for lecture dates.

Workshops

Gyleen Fitzgerald teaches workshops on colour and value in quilting. For workshop dates and to purchase a pattern, visit the web at www.ColourfulStitches.com. Discounts available to quilt shops.

Hand Dyeing

Colourful Stitches produces irresistible colour combinations. Our hand-dyeing process produces distinct, saturated colours, which are unobtainable in the commercial dyeing process. The end result is a 100% colour fast, washable, silky, drapeable scarf, pillow, or expressive cotton in colours to *dye* for!

Ordering Information

FPI Publishing books are available online or at your favorite bookstore.

Quantity discounts are available to qualifying institutions.

All FPI Publishing books are available to the booktrade and educators through all major wholesalers. For more information, visit:

www.ColourfulStitches.com

Colour Your World.

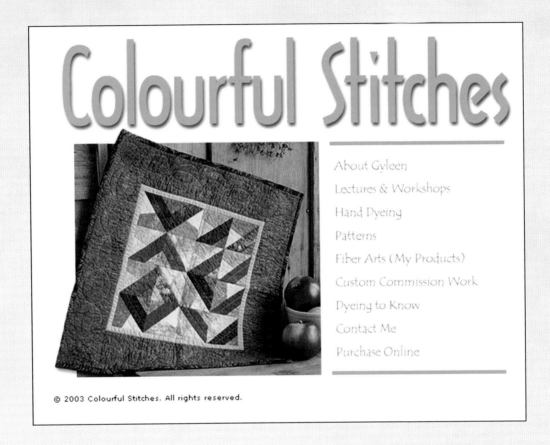

Gyleen is absolutely passionate about quilting!
Visit her on the web for patterns, notecards, signature
quilts, silk scarves and pillows, dinner napkins,
socks, workshops, lectures, and much more.

www.ColourfulStitches.com